A MODERN FAMILY

A MODERN FAMILY

Socrates Adams

Bluemoose

for my family

Copyright © Socrates Adams 2013

First published in 2013 by
Bluemoose Books Ltd
25 Sackville Street
Hebden Bridge
West Yorkshire
HX7 7DJ

www.bluemoosebooks.com

British Library Cataloguing-in-Publication data
A catalogue record for this book is available from the-British-Library

Paperback ISBN 978-0-9575497-0-8

Hardback   ISBN 978-0-9575497-1-5

Printed and bound in the UK by Short Run Press, Exeter

Part One

A television presenter drives around a town in England. He stops at red lights, beeps at inconsiderate drivers, correctly applies his brakes, accelerates efficiently, observes the highway code, considers suicide, steers, checks all three mirrors, starts, stops, moves. The television presenter imagines a handsome man driving a high-performance car down a road by an ocean in the sun. He doesn't care about whether or not he is that man. He imagines an ordinary man, driving a low-performance car down a road by a supermarket in bawling, growling rain. He doesn't care about whether or not he is that man.

He drives past a Tesco's. He drives past another supermarket. A small, sweet smelling cardboard pine tree dangles from his rearview mirror.

I need to get some shopping, he thinks. If he doesn't get shopping from a supermarket, his children will die of starvation. He doesn't want that to happen. He imagines his children playfully eating from steaming plates of food. He introduces his children to the audience of thirteen million, viewing at home. Time to shop, he thinks, happily.

He parks in a supermarket car park. Rain tracks down the windscreen. He grips the steering wheel a few times, happy that it yields slightly to the pressure. The dashboard of his car is a smiling face, helping him to express his emotions. He laughs to himself and feels fine. He takes the key out of the ignition.

A customer walks past the television presenter as he lopes through the shop entrance. The customer thinks, I recognise that man from the television. He looks worse in real life. He looks really awful in real life. The customer thinks briefly about asking for an autograph, but decides against it. A thick spray of water flies from the presenter's head as he shakes his long, grey locks. His scalp is visible through the hair, soaked to the skull. The customer goes about his business, getting into his car, driving home, and living the life of a customer.

Everything in the supermarket is covered in plastic. The presenter looks at the products on the shelves and thinks, I know what that is, or, what is that? He occasionally reaches out and touches something. Touching items in the supermarket provokes a melancholic surge which he cannot understand. He thinks, I am nothing, and goes on with his shopping. The aisles in the supermarket are badly organised. There's an aisle of cheap children's toys wedged between the meat and the dairy. The customers of the supermarket often think as they wander around, where is the item I'm looking for? The television presenter doesn't think this. His brain simply engages 'supermarket mode'. He walks up and down the aisles, basket in hand, feigning deep, passionate interest in products he sees; picking them up and setting them down at random with a sage look on his face, the look of a master chef, selecting the ingredients for a prize-winning banquet.

I Am Nothing, is the television presenter's default setting. He is so good at thinking it, there's nearly no effort whatsoever. He sometimes just feels that I Am Nothing is a kind of background radiation, an after effect of the big bang, like white noise on a television set. He thinks that without I Am Nothing there would be nothing. And that is major-league bull-shit, he thinks.

The television presenter first started thinking about things in terms of a type of league and some kind of shit a few years ago. One of his co-presenters had said 'that is major-league bull-crap' and he had found it very funny. He sometimes says, 'minor-league horse-crap,' or 'ultra-league crab-crap.' He just loves it.

What to make, what to make, what to make.

The great thing about food is that it is tasty, if you prepare it properly and make it from ingredients that you love to taste, says the presenter, to an audience of twelve and a half million at home. The presenter's hands finally alight on some pickled whelks and Irish soda bread. He cannot decide whether or not the children will like this for dinner. He thinks about buying more pickled things to match up with the whelks.

Once, the television presenter had presented a television programme from the seaside. He remembers the smell of the sea very vividly. He thinks that whelks, and other pickled fish are like the sea-in-a-tin. He takes his purchases to a counter. The cashier swipes his choices across the barcode reader. The presenter is waiting for the cashier to mention something about his left-field choices. Maybe he'll say something about how refreshing whelks are. Something about how the sour, complex notes of soda bread make it more interesting than standard, yeast-risen loaves. The cashier aggressively clears his throat, coughs painfully, wipes sweat from his forehead, hits his chest with a fist, and then whispers, almost imperceptibly, three pounds forty-three.

It takes the presenter four minutes to start his car. The rain has stopped. He turns on an uplifting CD of music from his youth.

On his drive home the presenter stops at some traffic lights. There is a lady at the traffic lights. He looks at the lady's buttocks. He turns up the music from his youth. He looks very hard at the lady's buttocks. He turns up the music so that it is very loud. He loves looking at the lady's buttocks. The lady's buttocks are his best friend. He looks at the lady's face. She is not looking at him. He turns the music up so that it is very, very loud. He opens the window of the car. The lady still looks away from him. He starts screaming along to the lyrics of the music. He screams and screams and finally the lady looks at him.

She sees an old man, beating his head in time to the music, screaming incoherently, opening and closing his window, being beeped at by other motorists. His eyes are wide open. He has long matted hair. She looks away.

The show is about high-performance cars. The cars scream around race tracks and fantastic international roads. The presenters of the show pat each other on the back and make jokes with each other. Sometimes, they look at each other and they are all thinking the same thing at the same moment. The thing they think is 'I hate you'. Then they make a joke about a car or some clothes or a haircut.

They re-booted the show a few years ago. The previous presenting team were getting old, and their banter was pretty weak. So in came the television presenter, the small one and the ugly one. Their on-screen chemistry is so fantastic that they often get viewing figures of thirteen or fourteen million.

Thirteen or fourteen million souls, sat quiet, hands on knees, teeth chattering with excitement and pleasure.

* * *

The table is laid for dinner: plates and knives and forks, spoons, glasses, fabric underneath it all. A child sits at one side of the table, another across from it, a wife and the television presenter, all sitting together wonderfully.

I bought pickled whelks and Irish soda bread for dinner, says the presenter.

He takes the items out of a white plastic bag and puts them onto the table. One of the children screws up her face. She is the oldest one. The best way to tell the children apart is that one is a boy and one is a girl. I don't want to eat that, she says. The wife looks over at the presenter and shrugs slightly. The other child is sitting at the table passively, looking straight ahead at the wall. He is thinking about school.

Please try and eat the pickled whelks and soda bread, says the presenter, tenderly. No chance, says the daughter. The wife is filing her nails. The presenter doesn't know what to do. He wants to do a television link at his daughter so that she will eat the whelks. This is Ellen, the best daughter in the world, he says to the audience of eleven million at home. She's about to eat her dinner, and it's going to be so outrageous that you won't be able to take your eyes off it. Ellen forks a whelk and looks at it, before it slaps wetly back down onto her plate.

The walls of the room are white, or off-white, depending on the light. The table is mahogany. Photographs of the television presenter meeting celebrities crowd the walls. A six inch by four inch family portrait sits on the mantelpiece. Sometimes the television presenter doesn't know whether or not the room is tasteful. He wonders whether if the room was more tastefully decorated, his daughter might be more inclined to eat her food.

I didn't do anything today except clean the house, says the wife of the presenter. The presenter is making a whelk and soda bread sandwich. No-one else is eating anything.

Did you enjoy cleaning the house Prudence, asks the presenter.

No, says Prudence.

Sorry about that. Maybe I should do some more cleaning of the house?

No, it's the only thing I have to do with my day.

You should take up a hobby. I've got my cars and of course I'll always have that. But what do you have? Bobby, tell your mother she should take up a hobby, says the presenter to the boy child.

Mum, take up a hobby, says Bobby.

Don't do everything your father tells you to, says his wife. She looks up from her plate and meets the eyes of the presenter. Your father is a silly man, she says, before starting to laugh. And he doesn't know what he is talking about, she says.

The presenter looks away from his wife, down at his whelk sandwich. He can hear his wife laughing and his daughter pushing whelks round her plate and his son saying, dad, mum says you are a silly man. He takes a bite from his sandwich. It tastes disgusting. His family don't eat anything. He keeps chewing and chewing the sandwich, not wanting to swallow the food, getting more and more frustrated, unable to think of anything apart from his inability to swallow.

Twenty minutes later, he orders three meat feast pizzas and his family eat them. He carries on eating pickled whelks on soda bread.

* * *

Guys, we need some great banter on this series of the show. You are all lads, so start acting like it, OK, says the director of the car show.

One of the presenters of the show says, that is super-league human shit, and laughs with the other two. Another of the presenters says, that is ultra-league cow poo, and the three of them laugh very hard together. The television presenter is nearly crying. He says, that is macro-league amoeba faeces. For some reason, no one laughs. The meeting room is silent. Two of the presenters and the director of the show all look at the other presenter.

The director writes down in his note book, 'POSSIBLE BANTER WEAK LINK.'

The television presenter gulps. He thinks, calmly, this is my life.

* * *

I recognise you from somewhere I think. Are you off the television, says the waitress. She is handing the television presenter a small glass of house red wine. He is asked something about being on television nearly every day. He sometimes wishes that being asked whether he was on television could be a sport or something, or some kind of hobby. He says, no, you must have me mistaken for someone else. I'm just a shopkeeper. I sell my organic vegetables every day. I do a veg-box delivery service.

It's a small, bohemian café, with hundreds of pictures of frogs and small statues of frogs everywhere you look. A lot of the frogs have lipstick on and one has a large curly moustache and is smoking a ceramic cigarette.

You look a lot like that guy from the car show on TV. You should be a look-a-like, you would make a lot of money, she says.

The waitress is cute. She is trying to be nice. The presenter just wants her to leave him alone. He wants to be able to cry into his glass of wine, or do something weirdly romantic or poetic with the wine, pour it over his heart or dunk his fingers into it and smear it across his forehead. The salt and pepper shakers on the table are two frogs, embracing.

Why isn't my agent here, he thinks to himself.

The waitress walks away from him and he looks at his watch. The watch is worth a lot of money. Someone gave it to him once because he posed for an advert. His picture went into a Japanese airline magazine, opposite a full page ad for a type of caviar that is harvested from eighty-year-old, albino sturgeons. He remembers the picture and thinks, I am old. His agent got him that advert. The slogan had been, A Modern Man.

The presenter's stomach feels empty and sharp. A sudden lick of acid rises up his throat, making him swallow frantically. He thinks that his heartburn is related to the fact that he is tired of waiting for his agent. He thinks about getting sick. He loves the idea. He thinks about working in a vegetable shop. There is a special on potatoes, he thinks. He wants to be a fat little Buddha in a vegetable shop. I put on four stone for this role, he says to the audience of five million at home, slapping his belly.

The agent strides through the tiny café, pumping the hands of the staff he meets and giving out business cards to whoever will take one. He fills the space of the entire café. The frogs seem to back slowly away from him, being consumed by the walls, floor, windows.

* * *

Bobby, son of a television presenter, is sitting in the school dining room, thinking about school work. It's a large octagonal room with high ceilings and many windows. He is eating a bowl full of custard. The table is a little small for him, his knees touch the underside of its surface.

A boy comes and sits next to him.

Bobby Martin, your dad is the one from that television show, isn't he, says the boy.

Fuck off, says Bobby.

Did you get expelled from your last school, asks the boy.

Bobby carries on eating custard from the bowl. He has only been at the school for a few days. The boy laughs a little bit. Bobby feels embarrassed. He can feel his cheeks turning red.

Leave me alone, he says.

Calm down Bobby, says the boy, we were excited about you coming to the school. Do you get to ride in fast cars sometimes?

I don't get to ride in fast cars. I don't even like fast cars. I don't like any cars.

Why not, says the boy.

Don't know, says Bobby.

Do you know who Harriet Gordon is?

No.

She's really fat.

Oh.

We're going to do something to her later. Do you want to join in?

Don't know, says Bobby.

* * *

Whenever the television presenter thinks about his career, he freezes inside and can't believe that he is alive, or that people have careers or care about them at all.

What new jobs are there for me, agent, says the presenter, my career is really important to me, as you know. You look ugly today.

8

They both laugh.

Banter is making fun of someone, to their face, so that they know it's only a joke, and they don't get upset about it, and then they do it back to you.

OK, good joke. Well, we have a few options. Car Mad, Car Mental, Cars on Tour, Car Squad, Mad Cars, Man Car, Male Car, It's A Man's Car, One Man and his Car and the High Powered Car Show, says the agent. Which one do you like the sound of and when can you start?

The television presenter doesn't want to do any of the jobs that the agent has listed. A waiter comes over to the table and asks whether the presenter is a presenter from television. He says no, and that he works in a vegetable shop.

Ha ha ha ha, says the agent, slapping the presenter on the back. He's just as funny and larger than life as he is on the telly, right? He slaps him on the back again. No, it really is the big-shot presenter that you think it is. He can sign his autograph if you like. I am his agent.

The presenter signs an autograph for the waiter on a napkin. It seems to him that the shapes that he has drawn on the napkin are not his signature, but an ancient symbol from a lost civilisation, a stamp from an office in a foreign country, a misprinted barcode.

The presenter begins to laugh and slowly, as his laughing becomes louder, the other diners in the restaurant become more and more quiet, until finally, everything sounds awful.

* * *

Here is a series of haiku poems written by Ellen, the daughter. She is sixteen years old and loves writing poetry. It helps her relax. She always leaves the first letters of her sentences in the lower case. She does it because she thinks that it makes all of the words as important as each other.

feeling young
although I don't know
nothing else

who am I
i have no idea
who I am

why do i
do the things i do
i don't know

She buys pale green, soft-back notebooks in packs of three from a local newsagent and fills them up with poems, diary entries and short stories. She has two brown boxes full of the notebooks. They are organised by date, theme and medium. Ellen likes to read through her old work every few months, moving the notebooks around depending on her changing tastes. She feels happy when she does this, even if she's cringing at some old, bad writing.

After carefully replacing the notebook of poems, she opens an older volume. She thumbs her way to the page she always looks at. It's all written in pencil.

What will I be when I grow up?

1. Lawyer. I would like to be a lawyer because I can help people and it's exciting.
2. Writer. I would like to be a writer because I like telling stories and playing imaginary games with my brother.
3. Hairdresser. I would like to be a hairdresser because my hairdresser is really nice.

She often still asks herself the question, what will I be when I grow up. Sometimes she can think of an answer immediately, sometimes it takes her a long time and she comes up with nothing at all.

When I grow up, I'm going to be exactly the same as I am now, Ellen thinks. I'm going to live with my parents until I'm eighty. My parents will die and I won't notice, and then I'll wander around the streets, trying to find new parents.

Ellen is checking her email. As she checks it, one of her friends sends her a message through gmail chat. They have this conversation:

tracy: hi ellen - your dad's on tv. the other two presenters are hot. can your dad get me to meet them?

ellen: haha that is sick.
no.
he can't get you to meet them.
you have really disgusting taste, tracy.

tracy: haha i would like to have sex with the small one
he looks like a rat
like a man-sized rat
that is hot
rats are hot
your dad is hot

ellen: fuck you

tracy: fuck you

They carry on chatting for around half an hour. Ellen does not feel comfortable talking sexually about her father's colleagues. Her friends often talk about her father's colleagues. She normally tries to turn her mind off while they do it. She concentrates on the sensations that her body is experiencing, in order to distance herself from processing the conversations she is having. She sometimes induces a heavy, trance-state in which she can think of almost nothing.

Bobby's English teacher has lined up the three guilty boys in the English office. She is walking in front of them and talking to them. She is asking about whether they think the way they acted is acceptable. She is asking them whether they would want someone else to do to them what they have done.

Bobby keeps thinking about Harriet Gordon, crying all of the time and having crumpled up paper thrown at her. She is the least popular girl in school. The children call her Fat Harriet. Bobby chewed the paper in his mouth before throwing it at her. Many spit-coated pellets were stuck to her back before she realised what they were doing.

The teacher tells the line-up of boys that they are torturing someone who has done nothing to them. Bobby does not feel guilty because of what he has done. He feels excited to be in trouble, and knows that talking to the other two about this experience afterwards will be fun.

Bobby Martin. Do not smile when I am telling you off, says the teacher. There is a look of calculated contempt on her face, her eyes oddly vulnerable at the same time as being sharp with anger. She is standing close to Bobby. He can smell vanilla on her skin. She looks straight into Bobby's brain and she says to it, I don't care who your father is, Bobby Martin, you are going to be punished for this.

The television presenter's son thinks, I am bored.

* * *

The school is almost empty and it's dark outside. There's a hollow silence in the warm office, filled occasionally by the short, angry sentences of Bobby's teacher.

The television presenter is finding it very hard to listen to the teacher as she tells him what his son has done. He is thinking about doing links for his television show. He is thinking about saying that certain cars are rubbish, or that certain other cars are not rubbish, that in fact they are very good, and that they can go at a certain number of miles per hour, or they can turn with authority, or precision, or character. He imagines being the size of a building and crushing cars with his bare hands before throwing them at his co-hosts. He wants to come back to school and go to TV presenting class. He wants to crawl into a womb and learn about life by watching Open University courses projected onto the soft pink wall. He is a luscious little foetus with a heart of gold and a trendy umbilical cord and amniotic sac twin-set with matching his and hers towels and a villa in southern Spain.

Bobby is a good boy, he says. The presenter is always amused by people accepting his hyper-stupidity.

He is not a good boy Mr. Martin. I am very, very worried about Bobby. He is a bully.

The teacher looks at the television presenter with large brown eyes. Her eyes say, I am serious.

He is just going through a tough stage, right, says the presenter.

It's something that needs to be acted on, before it gets out of hand. I am worried about the kind of example that you set him on your television show as well. What's the name of the small one on the show? He is always the butt of your jokes, and some of them can be quite cruel.

It's professional banter, he says.

It's cruel. I feel like your son needs a better role model. It's not helpful to have a father who is famous for being cruel to his co-presenters.

It's hot under the studio lights and the television presenter can feel the first tiny drops of sweat forming on his brow. Today we're going to play a traditional school playground game of tag, he says. He spins around and points at camera two. But with monster trucks, he says. The audience go wild.

I will talk to Bobby about this, says the presenter, he is a good boy. He just needs parental guidance.

Later on that day, the television presenter will try and talk to Bobby. He will keep losing interest and drifting off whenever he tries to talk to Bobby about his behaviour. His mind will keep returning to its normal state of natural, somnolent detachment. Bobby will not be interested, not feel threatened, not care about his father's concerns. Eventually Bobby will tell his father a joke about Fat Harriet and the television presenter will catch his eye for one second, smile briefly, and think 'major-league dog-shit'.

* * *

The wife of the television presenter knows nothing about Bobby's problems in school. She doesn't know anything about her daughter's poetry. She has no idea about her husband's concerns about his career. Prudence is always alone.

This egg is delicious, says her friend, sucking on a quail's egg.

They are eating together in a restaurant in an expensive area. They are eating quails' eggs that have been cooked with an extremely expensive mould.

It's heavenly, says Prudence. She can't taste anything. I never thought that I would hear myself saying that I like mould. But I love it. Look at me! I love mould. I absolutely love the taste of mould.

Her friend laughs. Prudence looks at her friend's nostrils. They flare up and then constrict. They do this over and over again. Prudence thinks about sphincters. Her friend carries on laughing.

Prudence and her friend meet up once a week. They discuss husbands, children, celebrities, culture, the economic situation, fear of Islam taking over the country, loss of traditional values, fear of young people, fear of getting old.

They meet in the mid morning, have cups of tea or coffee in a smart café. Then they head out to a fancy restaurant together. They love being waited on. Prudence doesn't enjoy their get-togethers at all. She hates drinking and eating, she hates talking to her friend. She hates her friend. Almost always, she goes to the toilet after eating the food, puts her finger down her throat, and tries to get sick. She never manages it, but awkwardly convulses into the toilet bowl over and over, staring at the small lake of contaminated water inches away from her face.

I always see Mark looking at other women, says Prudence's friend. It's disgusting. I see his eyes scanning up and down them, looking at their bodies. She is swallowing a piece of quail's egg. So I get my own back! I look at other men sometimes and think about them! Sexually! He has no idea about it.

That is really funny, says Prudence, not laughing. That's a really funny story. Prudence doesn't have sex. It's just a tiny chunk of experience that she has forgotten exists. The food in her mouth tastes of mulched autumn leaves. She imagines scooping leaves from the road with a long silver spoon, before sliding them into her mouth.

How are your children, asks the friend.

Oh, you know. They are little terrors, getting into scrapes, growing up, getting to the age when they start noticing people of the opposite sex, having an awkward adolescent time, just getting to know who they really are.

That is really funny, says the friend, without laughing. She doesn't have any children because her husband is impotent. Prudence often thinks that it is not worth talking about her problems with this particular friend, because she is a hateful, spiteful, bitter bitch. I am glad we are friends, says Prudence.

What would I do without you, says her friend.

What would I do without you, says Prudence.

You wouldn't be eating quails' eggs and mould, that's for sure, exclaims her friend.

They both set to the task of laughing heartily. Their laughter crashes awkwardly around the restaurant until they get bored and start eating another bite of egg.

I think I need a hobby, says Prudence.

You need an affair, says her friend, saucily. Prudence smiles and tries to seem conspiratorial. She remembers her life when she was a producer on a television programme. She thinks about it and misses it often. She remembers her interests and old hopes for the future. She remembers meeting the television presenter for the first time, and being excited by him. She remembers their first nights together. She remembers the feeling of being wanted. She remembers talking to him.

She remembers seeing a dull moon through windows as they lay naked, talking about the future. She remembers the texture of the wall as she touched it while they made love.

* * *

Mandy the producer is talking to the television presenter. He thinks that Mandy is a very intelligent and attractive young girl. She has a great talent for thinking up outrageous concepts for the show. Morris Minor pinball: Mandy's idea. Punto Pachinko: a great idea from Mandy. Every time the presenter thinks of an idea, his teammates say nothing for a bit and then burst out laughing. Or they just immediately say, no. His depression seems to be taking up a part of his brain that would normally control his skin, in some way. It feels like small, electric eddy currents are swirling around on his skin. He wants to peel it off, or, have it peeled off him by someone else.

Mandy, peel off my skin, says the television presenter. Just kidding, he says.

Mandy looks confused. She laughs a little in a nervous way. Mandy thinks, he is so weird. I definitely don't want to have sex with him, I guess.

Mandy is a confused young woman. She is not attracted to the television presenter, but feels like she should be. When she first met him, she thought to herself, oh no. I am going to end up having sex with this man, because he is a celebrity.

She was annoyed to discover that she could not force herself to feel any kind of lust for him at all. She tried reading about him on the internet, watching his show on repeat, buying annuals from the bookshop about him, masturbating about him and talking to him in a coquettish way. Nothing she does makes her feel horny or interested in him sexually. It makes her depressed.

She often sits at home watching repeats of the television show, crying and eating sticks of celery, wishing she could find a way to want to sleep with the presenter. Occasionally she writes ideas in a small, pale green notebook. She sucks the end of her pen and imagines what she looks like sucking it.

They are meant to be planning a special episode of the programme which is going to be filmed in a few months. The special will take place on "The Shittest Roads in The World". It will be an examination of the world's most dangerous, ugly, and boring roads. They are planning to go to some places in England, but mostly abroad.

Time for the production meeting, says Mandy.

The production room is too small for all of them, really. There's a huge pot plant in the corner that is bigger than the presenter. It looks a lot like a palm tree that's completely lost.

Let's get this show on the road, says the presenter. He makes this joke a lot. Mandy thinks it is not funny. She laughs all the way into the production meeting.

The other two presenters are there; the short one, and the ugly one. They are both sitting with their legs spread wide apart so that it looks like they need a lot of space for their penises. They look stupid, their knees almost touching.

The presenter sits down on his chair and crosses his legs. The other two presenters look at him and start snorting and snickering to each other.

What's the matter? Trying to hide your vagina from us or something, says the ugly one. The short one looks like he is going to start crying, or pass out due to lack of oxygen as he loses the ability to breathe because of violent laughter. The television presenter has two simultaneous fantasies. One is a fantasy in which he stabs both of the other presenters in their

17

hearts with an ice axe. The other is a fantasy in which he makes a great joke and they both laugh at it and pat him on the back.

Ha. No way. Good one, says the presenter. He uncrosses his legs and tries to move them as far apart from each other as he can. There is maybe a square foot of space in the room that isn't occupied by either leg or plant.

Mandy the producer talks to the presenters about the particular challenges of the upcoming special. Listening to her voice, the presenter becomes melancholy. He thinks about young women, and the start of his life. Welcome to This Is Your Life, says Michael Aspel, to the presenter. The audience at home is monstrously large. He stares at the pot plant, with a confused smile on his face.

Mandy looks at the television presenter. He looks like he hasn't noticed that she has noticed him staring into space. She doesn't know what to do. She imagines briefly waving or prodding the presenter, but instead she carries on with the meeting and tries to think of how she will ever be attracted to him.

* * *

One carrot. Three pieces of broccoli. A tomato. Three mushrooms. Acai berries. Crème fraiche. The blender goes on. Prudence is making smoothies.

The vegetables blend into a glutinous brown paste. It doesn't look good. Prudence thinks, needs more broccoli. She gets some more broccoli florets from the fridge, and drops them into the blender. The paste still looks brown. She looks at her collection of designer wine glasses. They are standing on a stainless steel shelf near the window. When sunlight comes into the room, the glasses look lovely.

She takes a glass from the shelf and tries to pour the smoothie into it. It takes a long time to come out. She has to shake the blender up and down to loosen it. With a sliming thump, the smoothie finally drops into the glass. It looks like shit.

Prudence thinks, this for breakfast, this for lunch, lean turkey steaks for dinner.

She sits down at the table and looks through some papers and magazines that happen to be on it, trying to put off drinking/eating the smoothie for as long as possible. She reads the back cover of her television magazine. The back cover is an advert for some plates that commemorate the imminent royal wedding. The plates look cheap. The pictures of William and Kate are badly drawn and lazily coloured. William looks a lot like Princess Diana in the picture. Prudence thinks, it's so cynical.

She picks up the phone and dials through to the sales office of the plate company. She orders the commemorative plate. It costs £29.99 and comes with a small, ornate spoon. Prudence can't wait for the plate to come so that she can invite someone over. The person she invites over will come over and have no idea about the plate and they will see it and then they will say, oh wow, Prudence, that's smart, and Prudence will say, you know, it's nice to be a part of history, and the person will say, yes it is.

Underneath the television magazine are school reports for Bobby and Ellen. Prudence starts reading the school reports but the words don't really make any impact on her. She skims over sections about Bobby having emotional problems and Ellen being introverted and quiet. She looks at tables which show effort and attainment for the two children. Here is Bobby's table:

Subject	Effort	Attainment
Maths	1	2
English	1	2
Science	1	2
French	1	2
Physical Education	5	2

There is a note to say that 1 = very poor and 5 = outstanding.

Here is Ellen's table:

Subject	Effort	Attainment
Maths	3	3
English	5	5
Science	2	3
French	2	3
Physical Education	1	1

Prudence thinks about what her report would say. She sketches out a table of effort and attainment:

Subject	Effort	Attainment
Cooking	5	1
Cleaning	5	1
Hobbies	0	0
Sex	1	1
Happiness	1000	-1000
Creativity	0	0
Financial Security	0	5000000000000

She writes a note at the bottom of her table to say that -1000 is very poor and 5000000000000 is outstanding. She looks at her table for five minutes or so, not feeling anything. She looks away from the table for five minutes or so. She looks back at the table and then at her smoothie, and then at the commemorative plate advert, at her phone and then straight up through the skylight at the clouds above her.

The clouds are ready to drop a batch of rain onto the country.

Prudence takes hold of the glass with her hand, which shakes wildly. It feels like her fingers are jumping between points in space that are metres apart. Prudence feels that each separate point in time is disconnected from the points that precede and follow it, forcing her body to shake in an unrealistic, disjointed way.

The glass at her lips, she tilts the paste into her mouth. It doesn't taste good. Some spills thickly down her chin and fibrous chunks fall onto her expensive top. She manages to swallow some. A lot is being spilled onto her face now. She decides to obey the will of whatever seems to be controlling her body and pours the rest of the smoothie over her head.

A thought happens to Prudence. The thought is:

You need to do something.

* * *

Ellen and Tracy sit together on a wall in the school. They are cold. They are eating lunch together. Tuna paste on brown bread with hula hoops and capri-sun. An apple with a cold, damp, bacon sandwich and supermarket own-brand brown sauce. Salt and vinegar squares. Their legs shake in the wind.

Ellen and Tracy go to a very expensive school for children whose parents are rich or famous or rich and famous. Tracy's mother is the British ambassador to Romania. Tracy often says that her mother and father are retards and that everyone in Romania is a retard. She very rarely gets to see her parents because they are usually in Romania. She lives with her grandmother who does not have anything to do with Romania. Tracy sometimes gets poppers and sniffs them and then giggles for about 30 seconds and then her nose bleeds. When she does this, Ellen watches her but doesn't join in. Tracy says, in between laughs, you are so boring, Ellen, I don't know why I hang out with you. Then Ellen says, because you fancy me, and laughs. Tracy laughs.

Ellen thinks that Tracy is the most beautiful and clever girl currently alive on the surface of the planet. They met on a morning of the second week of senior school. Ellen had been walking to school in inevitable September rain. She had heard quick footsteps behind her, and had turned to see Tracy, hurtling towards her, carrying a card folder above her head. Aren't you worried about getting the paper inside wet, asked Ellen. Tracy had just giggled a little and said, no.

Later, at the end of the day, walking home together, Tracy told Ellen how she'd tricked a teacher by telling him she'd fallen over and soaked her homework, so that it was totally unreadable.

Did you get the money for the gig tickets, says Tracy to Ellen.

No, says Ellen, and then, quietly, my mum is a bitch.

Ellen, you have to get the money. I don't care about your mum. Come on. It's going to be amazing. I've got something special planned. Tracy looks lovely. Her eyes are wide and she is pleading with Ellen. She says, ask your dad. Tell him that one of your friends will shag him for money.

The two girls laugh.

The bell for the end of lunch rings. Ellen takes a small, lacquered make-up case from her bag, and starts to lightly apply some powder to her cheeks.

When did you start wearing make-up, says Tracy. Ellen shrugs and blushes a little. A while ago, she says.

The two girls stand up, dust off the backsides of their skirts, pick up their lunch boxes and head into the classroom for the afternoon's lessons. Ellen thinks briefly about taking hold of Tracy's hand. She remembers a time when her mother held her hand. She becomes confused and decides she doesn't want to think about anything.

* * *

No, says the television presenter.

Bobby laughs at his sister.

Prudence sits at the table, thinking about doing something.

Dad, I really want to go, says Ellen.

Ellen, you are too young to go to gigs. Sixteen is too young.

You used to let me watch 15 certificate movies before I was 15, says Ellen, this is the same.

Prudence, what do you think about this, says the presenter.

Prudence looks at him for a moment. She is trying to think of the best thing to say. She puts her fork into a piece of lean turkey.

Will there be alcohol there, says Prudence.

Probably, but I don't drink.

Of course you don't drink – you are sixteen years old, says the presenter. Everything he says comes straight out of his mouth, without being processed by his brain.

If you give my sister money for a gig, I want money for sweets at break time, says Bobby. She always gets whatever she bloody wants.

Don't swear, Bobby, say Prudence and the presenter.

What's the name of the band you want to go and see?

They're called The Problem and they are really good.

The Problem are an OK band. Ellen thinks that they sound very similar to a lot of other bands and can't really understand why Tracy is obsessed with them. The lead singer of The Problem is very good looking, says Tracy. Ellen and Tracy at one point had a discussion about what sort of a penis he might have.

Tracy kept saying, I bet it's huge. Ellen kept saying, yeah, and thinking, this is boring.

Mum, Dad, I never do anything like this. My friends go out all the time, like, every weekend. I just sit in my room all the time.

It's easy to look good if you compare yourself to idiots, says the presenter, with a huge amount of relish. His father used to say the same thing to him before he became a rich and famous television presenter. He used to say to his father, look at all of those idiots going into their jobs, sweating in offices, being miserable. I am trying to do something with my life, and his father used to say, it's easy to look good when you compare yourself to idiots.

The television presenter feels good when he acts like his father. The times that he does are among the few moments in his life when he feels that he is definitely acting in an appropriate way, because that is the way that fathers are meant to act.

There are many psychopaths who will kill you also, says the presenter. It is dangerous being young and in a gig.

Nothing is going to happen to me. I am going to be fine. It's a safe place, and I am going to be with friends. Just let me go to the gig, please.

She is almost forcing herself to cry. She feels tears very nearly forming at the lower rim of her eyes, but she can't understand why. She does not feel sad, she does not feel angry, she doesn't even feel particularly frustrated. She starts crying.

Prudence is indifferent as to whether her daughter goes to the gig or not. The presenter is trying to act like a father, but doesn't really care whether Ellen goes or not. Bobby just wants to eat his dinner.

The television presenter sighs, building a relationship with the audience at home.

I'll give you the money, OK? Just take care of yourself. Don't drink any alcohol. Stay away from strange-looking men.

The presenter says this. He stops worrying about his daughter and starts thinking about the world's shittiest roads. His wife starts thinking about doing something. Ellen starts thinking about writing a poem. Bobby thinks about eating his dinner.

* * *

Inside Bobby's locker at school are two things.

1.   A 'mould farm'

2.   Ten pornographic magazines.

The 'mould farm' is in the top corner of his locker. Different types of food are spread across the metal of the locker, each coated with a different type of mould. Spindly white strands, rich black blooms and flattened velvet rolls, the powder blue colour of Wedgewood. The 'mould farm' smells disgusting. It means that the two boys who have lockers next to him do not ever use them. Sometimes he looks at the different types of mould that grow on the different types of food and thinks about how he would present a piece to camera about the mould. He imagines that he is his father, ranking the mould on appearance, rate of growth, value for money etc.

He tried to grow long hair like his father one year. A friend had said, why are you growing a mullet, and he had gone home that night and asked his parents to get his hair cut. His dad had said, about time – you don't want to grow a mullet like your old man.

Bobby had thought, why not, and had said, I know – no way dad. I don't want to look sad. Father and son had laughed about it. Father was thinking, I look sad, son was thinking, I love my father.

Bobby keeps his ten pornographic magazines in an A4 plastic wallet so that they do not get infested with mould spores. It doesn't stop them smelling awful.

He has taken time, at home, to separate each individual page of the pornographic magazine. He sells the pages for one pound each. A glossy cover of a magazine costs two pounds because of the high quality finish, and sexy writing. All of the children whose parents have put a block on adult internet sites buy the magazines from Bobby, who is the only boy brave enough to buy them from newsagents.

Once, Peter Yallop had asked Bobby to buy £30 worth of magazines from a newsagent. Bobby had refused as he felt as though Peter Yallop may have been trying to set up his own pornography trading business with the £30 initial stock.

Peter Yallop had gotten angry with Bobby and had attacked him, punching and kicking him in the shins and shoulders. Bobby had yelped and fallen to the ground. Bobby and Peter were no longer friends.

King George's school is a very respectable private school, set in four acres of picturesque grounds. The entire site is on the side of a steep hill.

The lockers are towards the bottom end of the school. The corridors are filthy round here and teachers rarely stray this far down from their staffroom. The children seem to be in charge.

A boy from Year Eight approaches Bobby at his locker.

Can I have a look, says the younger boy.

It's one pound per page. Let's see your money before I get it out, says Bobby.

The Year Eight boy takes one pound out of his pocket. He holds it up so that Bobby can see it. Bobby takes the pound from the other boy and puts it in his pocket. He turns around to his locker and takes the plastic wallet of pornographic images out. He selects a page which is 60% text and 40% images on one side, and full of adverts on the other. He gives the page to the boy.

Are you kidding me, says the boy, turning the page over a few times, there's almost no pictures, and this one's just a cock!

Bobby looks at the picture. It is a picture of a disgusting red penis entering a vagina.

There's penetration in that one. That normally costs more. You are lucky to get it.

I want tits, says the boy.

No, says Bobby, that's what you're getting, unless you have more money.

This is shit, says the younger boy, I'm going to tell everyone it's shit, and I'm going to tell a teacher about it.

Try if you want, says Bobby, do you know who my dad is?

Yes, everyone knows. It's not that amazing, Bobby Martin.

Bobby looks at the boy, with a calm face. He speaks, feeling detached from the meaning of the words that he says,

It means I can do whatever I want at this school, and I will never get into any trouble at all. Never. So you can tell whoever you want about whatever you want, and it will just get you in trouble, because you are the one who bought the porn, and I had nothing to do with it.

Bobby, angry, rips the page of the magazine out of the boys hands.

Get out of here, Bobby says.

Bobby watches the boy walking away from him and thinks about what he is going to do with the money he is making from all this porn. He feels ashamed.

* * *

I spend all of my time in my room, thinks Ellen. I suppose other people spend time in their rooms, or eating with their parents, or doing hobbies. My hobby is poems, which I do in my room.

Ellen opens a drawer of her desk and removes a stanley knife and a pencil. She cuts thick, satisfying curls of wood and graphite from the end of the pencil until she reveals a fantastically sharp point.

The point was in there all along, she thinks. Hiding, she thinks.

She writes one line of a haiku poem. The poem starts with the word, victory. She is listening to a song by the band The Problem. It's a song about being a young lad in the big city and having a drink with your friends while holding down a depressing nine to five minimum wage job. Ellen thinks that the song is a bit obvious, and very similar in style to a lot of other bands with similar names to The Problem. She thinks that if she was in a band she would write songs that were not about anything. She would think of beautiful sounds, or combinations of words that made no sense, just so that she was not writing just another gritty realist song.

I want to hear more music written by women, she thinks.

Ellen has a programme on her computer that automatically displays what music she is listening to as her gmail chat status. At the moment she is called:

Ellen Martin

>Fourteen by The Problem

A chat window pops up.

Tracy: AMAZING SONG

Ellen: haha

Tracy: going to listen to it

Ellen: its really good

Tracy: very excited about the gig – did you know laura went to a secret gig at tom's house????????

Tom's the lead singer of The Problem.

Ellen: you kidding me? how?????

Tracy: they sometimes post secret gig times on a secret message board – they do so much for their fans – cool

Ellen: i know – what's the plan for the gig?

Tracy: meet at 6 at my place – got some booze and stuff...

Ellen: ???

Tracy: it's going to be a GOOD night

Ellen is guessing that Tracy has got some kind of drug for them to take. She is scared. She's never taken drugs.

Ellen: its going to be great. know what your wearing?

Tracy: basically naked. i am going in fancy dress as a teenage slut

Ellen: same

Tracy: i wish i had your breasts

Ellen doesn't reply for a minute. She is blushing. She thinks about her breasts. She thinks about Tracy's breasts. Tracy has small breasts. She wears a small bra. Ellen's breasts are slightly larger than Tracy's. They are not much bigger. Ellen can't think of what to write. She feels confused. She thinks about Tracy wishing that she had her breasts. She wants to write, I wish I had your legs. She is too scared to write it.

Ellen: sorry! my dad just came in the room haha

Tracy: your dad is a weirdo

Ellen: fuck you

Tracy: haha

Ellen: can't wait for the gig – going to try and do some work – see you tomorrow x

Tracy: x x x

Ellen deletes the first word of her poem and replaces it with the word 'Tracy'. She writes a tender poem about her feelings. She writes four more poems that evening.

She does no work for school that evening.

Ellen dreams about Tracy that evening.

Ellen wakes up in the morning and feels guilty, and excited, and disgusted with herself. She feels like she doesn't want to go to school or eat her breakfast. She does both.

* * *

Prudence is looking at job websites. She has been working on her CV all morning, drinking coffee to try and get herself into a professional mood. She thinks, got to get my caffeine kick, as she drinks the coffee.

Yesterday, Prudence had cleared out a small spare bedroom in order to change it into a little office for herself. She'd moved boxes of the kids' baby clothes into the attic, and had cleared old school work and files from a dark wood roll-top desk. The single brass bed remained in the corner. Two of Ellen's old soft toys sit on the bed and watch her type and click, their black, button eyes grim and judgemental.

She is searching for jobs in the media, producing a show, or being an assistant producer; something that would be a challenge for her. There are not many jobs. She thinks that perhaps most of the jobs are advertised in trade papers, or on internal websites in the companies she'd be interested in.

There are some production jobs for internet companies and very small television channels. Prudence thinks that she would feel depressed working in a place like that. She thinks about the unglamorous presenters, and boring stories and shows she would have to work on. Her finger floats a little above the left mouse button.

She drinks more coffee.

She sends her CV to a lot of places. She has not worked for around sixteen years. She is forty seven years old. There is an immobilising feeling of desperation pressing down on Prudence. She pretends that she feels OK, occasionally, then realises that she does not feel OK. She has sent her CV to twenty different places. She thinks, that will do it.

She sends an email to her friend, with, Back in the Job Market, as the subject line. She writes the email in the most joyous, optimistic tone that she can manage. The more optimistically she writes, the more humiliated she feels. She writes the sentence, I am just so excited about all of this, it really feels like a new chapter in my life.

The doorbell rings.

Prudence thinks, that's weird. She can't imagine who it is at the door.

She looks at herself in the mirror on the way to the door. She looks OK. She looks like a forty seven year old housewife.

She looks through the peep-hole on the door. It is a delivery man. He is holding a package and a clipboard. The delivery man is handsome. He is wearing a baseball cap. Weird, thinks Prudence. A baseball cap, thinks Prudence.

She thinks, baseball cap, in utter dumbfounded incomprehension, around ten times, very quickly.

I suppose that's the world I live in now, she thinks.

Prudence opens the door.

Prudence Martin, asks the delivery man.

Yes. But I am not expecting a package.

Well, I've got one for you. He smiles a huge, gap-toothed grin. The delivery man has a name tag on. It says that he is called Jared.

Probably American, thinks Prudence.

Could you sign here?

He holds an electronic pad out toward Prudence.

Sure. Would you like a coffee? Prudence feels excited.

The delivery man looks calm and slightly confused. He does not look aroused.

No thank you, I'm in a bit of a hurry, says the delivery man. He holds the electronic pad closer to Prudence. He really wants her to sign it.

She signs the pad and takes the package from the delivery man. She says good-bye and closes the front door. Prudence had just wanted to give the delivery man a coffee and tell him that she was back in the job market. Oh, what type of job, the delivery man would have said. Nothing too crazy, just some television work, Prudence would have slyly replied, before adding, it's nowhere near as glamorous as you think.

She walks to the kitchen table and sits down. She opens the package. It is the commemorative plate for the royal wedding she ordered. It looks and feels very cheap. The painting is bad and the finish feels grainy and rough. She looks at young Kate Middleton on the plate and hates her. She looks at her apricot cheeks and her sweet, wholesome smile. She wants to be a home-wrecker. She wants to crawl into Prince William's bed while he's asleep and curl around his royal body.

Prudence Martin is all over the place.

She opens a new file on Microsoft Word. She calls the document: Prudence Martin is All Over The Place. She closes the programme, and when asked whether she wants to save the changes, she clicks No.

* * *

Ellen puts on lipstick. She looks at herself in the mirror as she does it. She looks good. She puts on eyeliner. She feels good. She can smell the make-up and it smells sweet.

She listens to old fashioned English folk music as she prepares to go to the gig. The singer sounds as beautiful as someone would sound if they were dying of a broken heart, she thinks. Ellen takes a small envelope out of her drawer. Inside the envelope is a birthday card that Tracy gave her last year.

Tracy's handwriting is large and looping, making the two 'l's in Ellen look like loosely coiled string. She doesn't open the card, but briefly plays with the envelope, before putting it back into the desk drawer. She doesn't need to read it, she has the card memorised, clear as a photograph in her mind:

Happy birthday Ellen. You owe me £10 for vodka money.

Tracy had given it to Ellen in front of Prudence and had said, go on, read it out, it's a nice message isn't it. Ellen had had to make up something on the spot. She'd said, happy birthday to Ellen, my best friend.

Tracy still teased her about it, a year later.

Ellen has never taken any sort of narcotic before. She has drunk alcohol, and she has smoked cigarettes. She has a third of a bottle of whisky in her cupboard, hidden from her mother. She wonders about what sort of drug Tracy has managed to get hold of. She spends fifteen minutes or so googling different drugs and their effects. As she comes across each one, she makes a mental note as to whether she would try it.

Cannabis – Yes

Cocaine – No

LSD – Can you even get that any more?

Magic Mushrooms – Yes (seems unlikely)

MDMA – No

Mephedrone – No

Opium – No

Mescaline – Yes (seems unlikely)

Morphine - No

Ecstasy – Maybe

Crack – No

Methylone - No
Heroin – No
Ketamine – No
Opiate Prescription Painkillers – Yes
Poppers – No
Ludes – (What are these?)
Speed - Yes
Barbituates – (Are these the same as ludes?)
Crystal Meth – Absolutely not

I hope that it's either mushrooms, speed, mescaline or cannabis, Ellen thinks. She looks at herself in the mirror and moves her hair around. She pouts. She feels embarrassed. She feels OK. She is fluttering around because she feels excited about going out this evening.

She is wearing a short skirt. It comes down to three inches above her knees. She doesn't feel sexy. There is half an hour before she needs to leave the house, but she is ready to go already.

She sits on her bed, with her hands underneath her legs, hoping for the time to pass quickly. After five minutes of waiting, she moves over to her stereo and turns up the volume of the music. A man is singing about something and it sounds good.

The whisky tastes of wood. She drinks a good mouthful. It just tastes of alcoholic wood, she thinks.

Ellen tries to feel hedonistic. She is playing loud music and drinking alcoholic wood juice. She tries to do some head-banging. She can't bang her head to folk music. She starts to listen to the most recent album of The Problem.

The first song is a spiky guitar song about sex. She drinks another mouthful of whisky and turns the music up and then hides the whisky in case her mother comes into her room.

Her bedroom is full of artefacts from her childhood. Not so many soft toys, but plenty of etch-a-sketch, lockable diaries, art kits and expensively papered notebooks. A lava lamp glows in a corner, and fairy lights hang from the ceiling, draped over a set of shelves. On the ceiling are glow-in-the-dark stars. She stares at them in the evening, tracing faces and shapes of exotic animals and places, waiting to sleep.

She decides to leave the house early, taking her coat from the cupboard and stashing the whisky in a smart grey bag. As she leaves her room she looks at her face again in the mirror.

I really do look OK today, she thinks.

She buys a packet of cigarettes from the shop and waits for Tracy in the middle of town for twenty minutes.

* * *

Bobby is in his room. The moon looms above his house and quiet animals stalk along tree branches nearby. His father is in the pub. His sister is at the gig. His mother is doing something else. Bobby Martin has a secret.

The walls of Bobby's room are covered in posters of his dad's car show. His dad always asks him whether he's getting a little too old for these now, and whether he'd like some more tasteful, framed pieces of art for the walls. Bobby always tells his dad that he can't be bothered, and that he doesn't care.

He presses the power switch of his computer and feels excited. He connects to the internet. He goes to the website http://eu.battle.net/wow/en/ and clicks on the account management button.

Bobby's heart is banging hard in excitement.

Bobby takes a World of Warcraft 60 day pre-paid play time card from the pocket inside his school blazer. He thinks about all of the pornography that he had to sell to make enough money to buy the 60 day pre-paid play card. Up until two months ago, he had used his father's credit card to pay for the game. Then the television presenter found out about it and signed up to an on-line authentication application which stopped Bobby fraudulently using his card. At first, Bobby had panicked. Then he had calmly thought of a way to carry on playing World of Warcraft.

Bobby looks at a photograph of his dad on the wall, younger than he is now. In the photo, his dad is standing in the middle of the ugly one and the short one, arms draped around their shoulders. The presenter has a goofy smile. At the bottom of the poster it says, The Slow One.

Bobby scratches off the panel on the back of the play card, and enters the numbers and letters into some boxes on the internet. He clicks a small box to say that he understands that by scratching off the panel on the back of the card, he has "used" the card, and is no longer eligible for a refund.

He clicks "enter code".

He types the long string of letters and number into a series of small white boxes on-line. He presses "enter".

In order to play the latest version of World of Warcraft, Bobby has to wait for 2.3GB of patch information to download. His family has a fibre-optic internet connection, so he doesn't have to wait long.

Bobby's computer makes small whirring noises as the data is downloaded and the patch is applied. Bobby has a private language that he doesn't use with anyone in the real world; secret words from World of Warcraft. The language includes words like patch, proc, spec, tank, rep grind, tabard, mark of valour, azeroth, tauren etc. Some of the words seem like they may have a meaning independent of World of Warcraft, but they don't to Bobby. Proc, he thinks.

He listens carefully to the noises of the computer and imagines small strips of light flying around inside. He clicks on to some World of Warcraft websites while still downloading and reads articles about the character class he plays in the game, and news about the world that he may have missed while he has been away.

There is a noise, outside his room. It is the noise of a mother, creeping around and turning lights on and off. Bobby freezes. His mother calls up to him, Bobby!

He doesn't say anything. He feels ashamed of himself. He wants to bully someone.

Bobby, his mother shouts, louder.

Yes, he says back, quietly.

Do you have any dirty clothes I can wash?

No.

He hears the staircase creak under his mother's footsteps. He clicks on the small button which minimizes the installation client on his desktop. It shoots to the bottom of his screen.

His door opens and his mother looks at him.

What are you doing, she says.

Working, says Bobby.

Prudence rampages around his room, opening and closing cupboards, scooping up dirty clothes and tossing them into a basket. Can't you do this yourself, she asks as she whirls around. She holds up a particularly dirty pair of underpants and looks angrily at Bobby and says, this is disgusting. Bobby is thinking about Azeroth. He is thinking about the interesting landscape and architecture of Azeroth, and how the different parts of it are much more interesting than real life.

Did you hear me, says Prudence, and looks hard at Bobby.

Bobby says nothing. He waits for his mother to stop looking at him, and leave his room, muttering. Prudence briefly worries about Bobby as she walks down the stairs, and then begins to worry about herself again.

Bobby's patch finishes downloading.

* * *

The barman of the Ram and Shackle is looking at the three television presenters. They are each drinking a pint of cheap lager. He is thinking that he would like them to have bought expensive Bavarian Wheat beer, or expensive and trendy Martini cocktails. And some crisps. And peanuts. He looks again at them and thinks, celebrities, they are disgraceful.

The barman had ordered a very expensive new quiz machine two weeks ago, so that if any high-rolling businessmen or rich celebrities came into the pub, they could spend a lot of money doing a quiz.

Just my luck that it hasn't arrived yet, he thinks. Will nothing ever go my way?

The barman wants to put his head underneath one of the beer taps and press down on the handle and let the beer go into his mouth and drink it, never mind the waste.

He thinks, fuck the waste.

He fantasises about putting his head under the beer tap every day. It is his life-long dream. He has never done it. The closest he has ever come was to accidentally spill some beer onto his hand. When he spilled it, he thought to himself, come on, do it, put your head under and start drinking, you own the place, come on, no one will notice, it will look like an accident.

The television presenter looks at the barman occasionally and thinks, weird guy.

Top-league mutton-turd, says the ugly one.

Platinum-league butt-crap, says the small one.

Mega-league child-shit, says the ugly one.

Diamond-league yeti-stool, says the small one.

They laugh and laugh.

Hey, remember the other day when he was trying to hide his vagina from us, says one of them.

They all laugh.

Good one. I don't have a vagina, says the presenter.

I am really looking forward to filming The Shittest Roads in the World, the ugly one says, it's going to get the adrenaline pumping like nothing we've ever done before.

Damn right, the small one agrees.

Remind me where we're going.

England, Scotland, Romania, Serbia.

We are jet-setting guys.

We are going to win an award for our television show.

We are popular with people of all demographics.

Laddie humour is harmless fun.

The television presenter is very worried about travelling abroad. Whenever he has travelled abroad with the other two before, bad things have happened. They always say to him before they leave, what happens on tour, stays on tour.

He knows that means that something very bad is going to happen on tour. Normally it involves women with no clothes on. The television presenter will often not be able to sleep at night. He will think about what happened on tour.

The ugly one finishes his drink and moves to the bar. He asks the barman for three more cheap beers. He also asks for three cheap glasses of whisky and three cheap bags of peanuts.

The presenter drinks his cheap lager and cheap whisky. His colleagues buy more cheap lager and more cheap whisky. They talk about their families and their wives and their houses and their mortgages and he wants to fold himself up into smaller and smaller pieces, like a crisp packet in the hands of an anxious drinker. Many hours later, when nearly no-one else is left, he stops talking to the small one and the ugly one. He can barely see them. He just sees patterns of light reflected and refracted through glasses and mirrors in the pub. He laughs at the lights, somehow finding their way from the sun, to his brain.

He sees his own face in the mirror behind the bar and he stops still, stops laughing, stops everything and looks at himself intensely. He looks like a boy.

* * *

There is a low, erotic throb in the bar, under Ellen's feet. It is under the feet and around the body of every person in the bar. The music is loud. It is seriously loud. Everything is harsh in here, coated in acid and fire. The red and white light from the stage, the elbows of dancers, the cries of drinks orders at the bar.

This is the first support band. They play for twenty minutes. Tracy and Ellen are towards the back of the room. They try and talk to each other but neither can understand the other over the music. Occasionally, Tracy wild-eyedly thrashes her head around, before looking at Ellen, grinning, and squeezing her hand. Ellen feels excited whenever Tracy squeezes her hand.

When the support band finish, Tracy and Ellen try to make their way to the bar, through the crowds. Eventually they buy a drink each, and find an empty area to sit in.

What did you think of them, asks Tracy.

Amazing, Ellen replies.

They take sips from their drinks.

I am pretty fucked, says Ellen.

No no no, we're just getting started, says Tracy. Come to the toilet with me.

She grabs Ellen's hand, downs the rest of her drink, and pulls her friend along to the toilet with her. The toilet smells of a toilet. People have written graffiti all over the inside of the cubicle. A lot of the graffiti is swear words. Some of it is little phrases that make no sense. Some of it is illuminati signs. Some of it is pictures of a penis. The two girls laugh to each other.

Tracy takes a small burgundy purse out of her bag and takes out a small container. From the container she takes two scrunched up pieces of cigarette paper.

What is that, says Ellen. She moves some hair from her eyes and tries to look excited.

Just take it with me, says Tracy, looking reassuring. Ellen thinks about Tracy with her folder held over her head in the rain.

She smiles and feels nervous. What is that, Tracy, she asks.

Tracy looks at Ellen with very tender, loving, friendly eyes. She says, Trust me. We'll take one each.

Ellen feels terrified. She looks at Tracy and wants to kiss her. She wants to touch Tracy's face with her hands and then touch her lips to Tracy's lips. I wish I had your lips. Ellen puts her hand out so that it is underneath Tracy's. Ellen's best friend lets the tiny rizla packet fall into her hand. Feels heavy.

Tracy smiles at Ellen, puts her little packet in her mouth, and takes a long drink from her bottle. There is light. It pours down Tracy's throat. Ellen can see it, and wants to touch it.

She looks at the small wrap in her hand, and looks at Tracy's face. She puts the packet in her mouth and swallows it. It is quite tough to swallow. She takes a drink. She doesn't feel any light in her throat. Just a scratchy rizla, making her want to cough.

I hate people, you know? I hate them. I hate people, says Tracy. Ellen feels like blushing. She thinks about the things that Tracy sometimes tells her about her life at home. She doesn't feel any different yet. I love you, says Tracy.

I know, says Ellen.

* * *

A strangely serene night is broken apart by the television presenter. He is walking home, listening to loud prog rock on his ipod. Every few hundred metres he stops and thrusts both arms in the air, before mouthing passionately along to the chorus of one of the songs.

It's late.

His phone keeps buzzing in his pocket. There are messages from his wife on the phone that he hasn't read. He will read them tomorrow morning, hungover, and feeling guilty while Prudence still sleeps.

He pulls a leaf from a tree and looks at it in the orange street-light as he walks along. He methodically pulls apart the leaf, section by section, stripping the papery flesh away from its thin veins. He ends up holding just the central vein of the leaf before discarding it and taking another leaf from another tree.

The television presenter is very drunk.

His brain is not storing anything that happens to him as memories. Every action he takes is totally unprocessed by his brain.

It takes him four minutes to open his front door.

It takes him forty seconds to turn his burglar alarm off.

His wife wakes up. She comes downstairs and looks at the television presenter. Ten seconds later, she is joined by Bobby, who has minimised his World of Warcraft window so that he can see what is going on. Bobby starts laughing.

Dad, you are so drunk, he exclaims.

I'm just tired, Bobby, the presenter replies.

A particularly loud section of music is audible, rasping and tinny, through his dangling earphones.

You're wasted, Bobby says.

Prudence looks at the television presenter.

The television presenter has his shoulders hunched forward. His head is lolling around. He takes uncertain steps forward and back.

Go back to bed, Bobby, says Prudence, sternly.

Bobby heads up the stairs. At the top of the stairs he turns to look at his father again. He says, Dad, you are so cool. He thinks, Dad is a level 85 Dwarven Warrior.

The presenter doesn't notice what Bobby says. He is looking at his wife and wishing that she was Mandy the producer. He wishes his wife was encouraging and forgiving like Mandy. He wishes his wife didn't know him, so that she could forgive him.

Prudence waits for Bobby to go to his room. She looks at the presenter and says, what are you doing?

The presenter doesn't say anything. He looks up from the ground at his wife. He thinks about what he could say to his wife. He thinks about telling her that he has been celebrating with his colleagues. He thinks about telling her about The World's Shittest Roads. He thinks about telling her about the fun he had had while walking home with the leaves. He thinks about telling her about his existential crises. He thinks about telling her that he wants to talk about their relationship. He thinks about telling her that he is worried about Bobby and Ellen. Everything that he thinks of makes him feel more and more ridiculous. He can't speak. He feels as though he will never be able to explain anything about himself to anyone else, ever.

Prudence waits for the television presenter to do something.

The television presenter starts grinning at his wife. He moves his hands up to the sides of his body. He grins. His hair is a mess. He starts to slowly, rhythmically dance. He winds his arms around his body and moves his hips from side to side. His legs sway left and right. He makes a musical noise from his mouth. He keeps dancing.

Prudence wants to cry. She watches him wordlessly dance for a short amount of time before turning around and walking up to her bed. Ellen is not home yet, she thinks. She starts crying halfway up the stairs. She sees the commemorative plate and wants to smash it.

Ten minutes later, as Prudence cries into her pillow, the television presenter vomits for the audience of fourteen million watching at home.

* * *

Ellen loves Tracy. She loves the band. She is on drugs. She is dancing, in a way. There are too many other people around her to dance properly. She moves left and right a little bit, and moves up and down. To her it feels as though she is moving a lot, and very beautifully. She looks a lot at Tracy, feeling like she is disconnected from normal existence. Tracy pirouettes around serenely, wafting her unctuous beauty around Ellen, folding her into a caramel and meringue bed, kissing her with her arms and legs.

The lead singer of the band is watching Ellen as he plays the music. He groans and sings a little bit. He whips his hair back occasionally and grips the microphone stand. Ellen is oblivious to this. She perceives the music only as a part of her own thought processes, and is unaware of the existence of the singer. The band keep playing until they finish, do an encore and then leave the stage.

Ellen and Tracy carry on dancing to the music that the DJ plays. The feelings Ellen is experiencing seem like foreign exchange students. She feels happy and excited. Don't these students know that that isn't the way we do things round here, Ellen thinks, smiling to herself.

An hour later, nearly everyone has left the club, but Ellen and Tracy are still there, dancing. It doesn't seem like a harsh place now, but soft, and round. The lead singer of the band comes out of the backstage area. A lot of the crowd look at him and are impressed. Ellen doesn't notice, but Tracy sees him and is impressed and on drugs.

He moves toward Ellen and stands very close to her. She notices him. He says, Hi, do you want to come backstage? Ellen does not hear him and moves closer to him so that they can talk. He says do you want to come backstage? Ellen looks at Tracy. Tracy looks maniacally excited. She is almost jumping up and down. Ellen doesn't want to go backstage. She wants to carry on dancing here for two more hours until she is no longer on drugs and then go and buy something to eat and then go home and dream about Tracy and then wake up and feel guilty about taking the drugs and then live out her normal life.

Yes, of course, let's go backstage. She says. The lead singer of the band takes hold of her hand. It feels OK, because of the drugs. She has a very dirty erotic thought about Tracy. She tries to think the dirty erotic thought about the lead singer of the band. She can't.

Backstage the music from the DJ is less loud, and the other band members are drinking beer and lolling about. They take drugs from the top of a silver tray and talk and laugh about the gig and about the music. As Tracy and Ellen walk over with the lead singer, the other band members look up from their sofas and drugs tray and look lustfully at the two young girls, before making more jokes, drinking more beer and lounging on the sofas. The lead singer points to a sofa. Tracy and Ellen sit on the sofa.

It is cold and bleak in this room, thinks Ellen. Another wave of drug effect hits her, and she thinks, hello world.

Half an hour passes, and the lead singer pays a lot of attention to Ellen, and says almost nothing to Tracy. He keeps telling Ellen that she should be a model, and that he knows a model scout who she should talk to. And he keeps putting his hand on her leg and moving it around a bit. Ellen feels weird. She looks at Tracy as the lead singer moves his hand quite high up her leg. Tracy looks like she is going to explode. She says, Ellen, I need the toilet, come with me.

In the cubicle, the two girls have an excited conversation. Tracy repeatedly tells Ellen that the lead singer is clearly interested in her sexually. She says, he is so beautiful. Ellen thinks that she is not interested and then repeatedly says, I can't believe this is happening. They look at each other's backstage lanyard and giggle and hug each other. Tracy says that Ellen should try and shag, if not at least kiss the lead singer. She says that Ellen should give him a blow job and hand job. Tracy says that she would do anything to have sex with the lead singer. As Tracy says more and more things about having sex with the lead singer, Ellen feels less and less in control of herself. She feels almost entirely detached from existence. She watches herself giggle in the toilet. She watches herself applying more lipstick and falling about and feeling weird. She watches Tracy draw a bright red lipstick heart on Ellen's upper left arm. She feels herself having sensations in a controlled way. She manages her out of control feelings in a very effective way. She knows that she is going to watch herself have sex with the lead singer. She is going to watch herself lead the modern existence of a young person achieving all of their dreams and take life by the scruff of the neck. She watches herself, crying, and she laughs.

* * *

The two of them sit on opposite ends of the bed. Early morning light picks out details and imperfections in the room; a small crack in the ceiling, a missing section of skirting board.

I don't remember dancing. I'm sorry. I don't know why I did that. I love you.

Prudence is crying. The presenter is talking to her, trying to make her feel better. He thinks, it is my right as a conscious being to act in any way that I want.

He is hungover and feels disconnected from life.

The children are at school. Prudence is shaking her head. She says, I didn't know where you were. Prudence thinks about how she would feel if her husband were to be run over or stabbed in a pub brawl. She thinks, don't care, and I would get money.

We were celebrating this new idea we have had for doing a show. It's going to be about the world's shittest roads. It's called The Shittest Roads in the World. It's going to be a ground-breaking feature. I'm really excited. We are all really excited. Would you like to come to the shoot with me? We are travelling all over the world to Romania and Siberia and Scotland.

There is an odd, gaseous freedom to his questions and revelations. He is hungover. He doesn't worry about what he is saying, or his wife's reactions to what he says.

Prudence thinks that it is unusual for her husband to tell her anything about his work. She turns to look at him. He looks very messy and red eyed. Prudence feels tender and distraught.

You never tell me about anything that you are doing, she says to him, I feel as though we are living two separate lives.

I'm sorry that it feels that way.

I don't remember the last time we talked about anything.

I don't remember anything.

I don't know what we are doing.

I don't know anything about our children.

I feel lost.

I feel lost.

45

Prudence moves to the other end of the bed and sits next to the presenter. She looks at him and then takes hold of his hand. She holds his hand and thinks about what it feels like, and what it means. Prudence is emotionally drained. The presenter is hungover.

They sit next to each other, thinking about each other for a few minutes.

The television presenter says, the other two presenters bully me at work.

I thought that you and the ugly one bullied the small one.

No. That is just professional banter. The other two really bully me. They don't ever laugh at my jokes. They say that I have a vagina. They make me feel very bad about myself.

The television presenter feels a wonderful thrill as he realises that he is really speaking to his wife.

That's awful. Why don't you say something to them? Or to your producer?

The presenter thinks about Mandy, opening her notebook of show ideas, too busy to worry about his problems. He doesn't want to think about the other two.

No, they would just bully me more. That's the kind of thing that gets me bullied.

Darling, you have to do something about it.

I don't know what I can do about it. My agent won't find me any work that isn't to do with cars or lads, or lads going mental about cars. I need to stay in the job. It is helping to talk to you about it though.

I love it, says Prudence. She squeezes his hand and it sends a hot, vulnerable feeling of joy bouncing around the presenter's body. He looks at his wife and thinks that she is beautiful. He doesn't think about audiences or anything other than his wife.

Hey, says Prudence.

Yes, says her husband.

I hate my best friend. She smiles at him.

In the evening, the television presenter and Prudence have sex for the first time in over a year. They both have successful orgasms, for the first time in over two years. They both feel happy, for the first time in over five years. The television presenter is still tired from his hangover, and Prudence is still recovering from her emotional draining. They fall asleep with their bodies connected. They sleep through the night. In the morning, the television presenter wakes up and gets ready for work. He is not hungover any more. He thinks about the day ahead of him. He thinks about his children. He thinks about his car. He thinks about his agent. He doesn't wake his wife.

He stares for forty seconds at Prudence, sleeping. He thinks very hard, do something. He looks again at Prudence. He turns away. He leaves the room, turns towards the stairs, and smiles at the camera.

Part Two

This is the shittest road in Serbia, says the television presenter. He is standing next to a roadside memorial. The memorial is made from metal that has rusted. It is a 3ft tower with a glass door which opens into a tiny space in which a large candle is burning. The candle flame flickers in the wind, quietly remembering someone's life. People in Serbia can't drive, says the television presenter, but even if they could, they wouldn't be able to, because the roads are so bad.

The ugly one walks into shot and says, the roads in Serbia are mondo-league twat crap. The little one creeps into shot and looks up at the ugly one, who hits him in the face with a cap.

As you can see, there is virtually no concrete or asphalt, or tarmac or anything on this road, says the small one, rubbing his head. The road's surface is crumbed soil, hairs from stray animals, bone dust and small rocks.

And that's why we are going to have a race on it, says the television presenter.

Because it's dangerous, says the ugly one, with his trademark masculine intonation. He looks at the camera for five seconds, and then looks into the face of the man operating the camera.

Got it? he asks.

Yeah, says the cameraman. He takes a small cloth from his pocket and mops his brow.

You sweaty bastard, says the ugly one.

The cameraman laughs.

You fat fucker, says the small one.

The cameraman laughs.

The television presenter doesn't say anything. He looks at the two other ones and the cameraman. He wants to do banter at him. He can't think of anything to say.

Mandy the producer is standing behind him. He wants to impress her.

The presenter remembers back to the plane ride over here. Gin and tonic, sour cream pretzels; watching the BBC's international news. He had sat next to Mandy on the plane. He'd tried talking to her about her life a little, but she hadn't said much, talking mostly about ideas for new shows, and asking the presenter questions about himself. I'm just an average guy, he'd kept saying. I just lucked out in life, he had said. It's important for Mandy to know I'm not just an average guy. She has to know how special I am.

He thinks about going back in time and writing a script for himself to use in this situation. He thinks about spending a long time writing very detailed scripts for use in the rest of his life, trying to imagine every possible situation into which he could get.

The ugly one and the small one look at the presenter, trying to think of something. They look at each other and start laughing.

Good one guys, he says.

Good what, says the ugly one.

Good joke, he says.

You're the joke, says the small one.

Good one, he says.

The small one and the ugly one laugh at him. He imagines them tugging each other's penises and ejaculating.

I am going back to the hotel, he says, I want to be well rested for the race tomorrow.

The race tomorrow will be scripted. Because the television presenter has a reputation for being the slowest of all of the presenters, he will appear to be winning the race for a long stretch of time, before having a problem with the motor of his car which limits his speed to one mile per hour. He will then have to drive at one mile per hour for four hours to finish the race. That is the concept for the 'Shittest Roads in the World' episode.

A lot of the episodes play on the idea that he is the slowest of all of the presenters. He doesn't care about being the slowest. His agent always says, It's your thing, and then orders more food.

He imagines the audience secretly willing him on, trying to make him become the fast one instead of the slow one.

It is hot and dry in Serbia. Small clouds blow aimlessly around the sky, not knowing what they are doing. Small pieces of dirt blow around the road, not knowing what they are doing.

I am better than those cloud bitches and those pieces of dirt bitches, thinks the presenter.

He gets into his car and drives to Belgrade, the audience at home cheering and clapping his powerful turn of speed.

* * *

The pharmacist is an old lady with glasses on. She tells Ellen that she needs to see the doctor before she can sell her that particular medicine. She tells Ellen not to worry though because there is a doctor in this chemist who can see her in about five minutes. She asks whether Ellen's boyfriend is in the shop, whether he came with her?

No, says Ellen. She thinks that if she was in a film, she would say, I don't have a boyfriend. But she doesn't say that.

OK, well if you just want to sit down here, the doctor will be out to see you in a minute.

Ellen sits down on a small plastic chair. The chair is the same shape as the chairs that they have in schools. It has a sort-of-rectangular hole in the back of it, and is uncomfortable. Her knees touch together. She has a drugs hangover. She feels as though her body is on autopilot still. The green cross of the pharmacist seems to be everywhere that Ellen looks.

Ellen wonders if this doctor only deals with this particular type of consultation. She wonders about how many people come in to the pharmacist asking about this. She looks at a ninety-year-old woman sitting in a chair across from her and imagines the ninety-year-old taking drugs and having unprotected sex with a rock star. The old lady is drooling. Must have been mind-blowing sex, Ellen thinks. If Tracy were here, Ellen would say that to her. She would say, That lady is in for the same reason as me. Then she would pause. Then she would say, except she had a threesome.

The doctor walks out of his consultation room. He is a young, handsome doctor, holding a tidy clipboard.

Ellen? he says.

He holds the door open as Ellen stands, walks, enters and then sits.

When did you have sex with your boyfriend? Was it yesterday?

Yes.

Did you use protection?

The condom broke.

Really?

Yes.

Have you ever taken this medicine before?

No.

Have you been bleeding from your vagina at all?

Why is he asking me that?

You mean a period?

No, I mean, extra, unusual bleeding. More than normal.

No. It only happened yesterday.

The doctor asks some more odd questions. It looks to Ellen like he is just on a website, reading questions off it. After asking her each question, the doctor types more into the computer. She thinks that maybe doctors are just trained to use Wikipedia nowadays.

When the doctor is satisfied, he writes a prescription for Levonelle 1500.

You have to take it in front of me, the doctor says.

What, says Ellen.

The doctor opens a drawer with his back turned to Ellen. When he turns back, he's holding a little box and a paper cup.

Here's some water, you have to take the pill in front of me. It's so you're not building up a stockpile at home to use instead of normal contraception. Don't tuck it into your cheek and save it for later, I'll know.

Ellen removes the packaging and pops the single, large pill out of its blister. Seems like a lot of packaging for just one pill, she thinks. The pill goes down easy.

On the way home from the pharmacy she sends Tracy a text message which says, I did it.

Tracy doesn't reply for a long time. When the text finally comes, it says, I feel like shit.

* * *

Bobby clicks the 'New Character' button. He chooses the Alliance, and then chooses the Dwarf race. Bobby decides that he would like to be a warrior, as warriors can either be a DPS or Tanking class in World of Warcraft, and he will be happy doing either of those roles. He doesn't like the idea of being a healer, as it can be quite stressful at end-game, and everyone is very quick to blame the healer if the raid wipes.

He customizes his character, scrolling through various faces, hairstyles and hair colours, until he is relatively happy. He is not too bothered about the haircut, as for a small amount of in-game currency, characters can visit a barber in Ironforge. I think you even get an achievement for having a haircut, thinks Bobby.

He names the character 'BeefBeefBeef' because he thinks that it is a strong, funny name. Bobby laughs about the name.

He clicks 'Create Character'. The name is already taken, he is told.

Bobby thinks for a short while about other names he could call his character. He thinks about 'The Destroyer'. He thinks about 'Muscles'. He sighs and thinks that he can't think of anything good. He wants to call the character 'Arnold Schwarzenegger'. But that is not allowed, and also it would be too long anyway.

Eventually Bobby just calls the character 'MrMartin'.

Loading...loading...loading.

A short animated sequence plays. It describes some of the problems that the dwarves of Dun Morogh face in their daily lives in the World of Warcraft. Finally, the camera comes to settle behind a stocky red haired dwarf.

The world is covered in snow. Bobby's feet leave small footprints in the snow. Smoke rises from dwellings. The sun shines above. Tiny rabbits hop through the snow. Wolves stalk their prey all around. Bobby's breath condenses in the air in front of his mouth. A large yellow exclamation mark floats impressively above the head of a rugged looking dwarf in front of him.

Bobby crunches forward through the snow and talks to the worried dwarf. The local wolf population has seen a recent spike in numbers. Someone needs to do something about it. Bobby feels as though he could be up to the challenge. He feels the weight of the sword in his hand, and imagines hitting a wolf with it.

He accepts the quest.

He sees a wolf. He runs to the wolf and attacks it with his sword. When he hits the wolf, it does not bleed. Large white numbers are emitted from the top of the wolf. They hang brightly in the sky for less than a second, and then fade into nothingness. Occasionally, the numbers are slightly higher than normal, and are coloured yellow. Soon, the wolf falls down dead. Bobby searches its corpse, and finds a pair of cloth shoes hidden on it. He puts on the shoes. He makes a note, mentally, that he has killed one wolf. He has to kill five more, he thinks.

He kills five more, occasionally ripping the fangs from a corpse, or skinning it, or discovering a health potion on it. Bobby feels alive. He runs back to the dwarf who gave him the quest, and he lets him know that the wolf population is now under control. Bobby receives a sum of money from the dwarf and feels as though he has gained experience which will somehow make him stronger.

Bobby's body is briefly bathed in a shining golden light. He has reached level 2.

* * *

The antique phone continues to ring until Prudence, stumbling oddly, manages to lift the receiver. She is wearing her pyjamas. For the past five days she has not got dressed until five minutes before the children are due back from school.

Hello, she says.

Hello, is this Prudence? says someone.

Yes.

Prudence, this is Arnold calling from Bidding.tv.

Prudence feels more alert.

Oh. I mean. Hello. Arnold. Sorry, I was in the middle of something, and normally when someone calls for me it's a salesperson. My name's on all the bills ha ha.

Don't say too much Prudence, Prudence thinks desperately. Calm down Prudence, Prudence thinks to herself.

Ha ha, says the person on the phone. Well – I am a salesman! We all are here at Bidding.tv, in our own way ha ha.

Ha ha, says Prudence, happily.

I'm calling because we have your CV here, and we are very impressed.

Thank you, says Prudence.

We'd like to invite you in for an interview – that is if you haven't got another job already and if you are still interested.

Yes! says Prudence, I am interested – I can come in whenever you like. I mean, in the day time, that is.

Prudence feels stupid about saying 'in the day time'. She thinks very quickly in a recognisable 'I have thought this many times before so I don't need to process the thoughts' sort of way 'isn't it amazing that no matter how old you get you still say stupid things almost constantly in situations which feel stressful.'

Yes, day time suits me fine, says Arnold in an encouraging way.

They arrange a time that is convenient. Prudence feels very excited throughout the conversation. She thinks about Kate Middleton. She thinks about a plate to commemorate her interview. The plate would have Prudence's face on and it would say at the bottom 'Interview' and Prudence's face would be badly drawn by an artist and only vaguely resemble Prudence.

After the phone call, Prudence pumps her fist in the air and says 'Yes' and then takes her pyjamas off. She is naked and walks around the house. She walks into all of the rooms of the house, smiling. In each room she thinks, 'Fuck you, life,' and feels excited. She stands in front of the mirror in the bathroom and looks at herself. She thinks that she looks good. She puts on a nice outfit and feels good. She walks into town and goes to a bookshop.

She buys a copy of *You're Hired! Interview: Tips and techniques for a brilliant interview* and sits in the coffee shop with a coffee and piece of cake and her book and feels great.

She reads about interviews and starts to feel confident. She's slowly remembering what it feels like to work in an office. She remembers what it's like to talk to people in the daytime, instead of being at home, watching television and drinking smoothies. She has never really watched Bidding.tv before, but feels as though it is just a normal television shopping channel. She thinks that it doesn't really matter to her what type of channel she works for, or job that she does, she is just happy to have the chance to do anything. Prudence thinks about how unimportant her life is compared to Kate Middleton's. Prudence is depressed. She feels great about her opportunity. She stares ahead at the wall of the café and wishes that she was nothing. She looks at her cake and feels mentally drained. She just wants to be Kate Middleton. Kate Middleton hovers in front of her, brilliantly, shining in her normal-girl-gone-great magnificence. Kate Middleton is the only good woman currently in existence and she is not a TV producer. The only way to be a good woman is to be young and be getting married, thinks Prudence, and then hates herself for it. She hates nothing.

Prudence is just a working mother trying to find fulfilment, trying to please her man, trying to raise her kids for fuck's sake. She is a 9-5 mom with a great heart. Prudence wishes she was Kate Middleton and eats her cake and doesn't understand anything. She can't wait for her interview.

* * *

It is a hot and dusty night in Belgrade. Serbians walk into shops and bars and their houses. The television presenter sits at the bar in his hotel thinking about racing. He looks occasionally at the barmaid who moves from side to side almost constantly for no reason. He thinks about his wife.

There is a song playing over the stereo system in the bar. He can't understand the words of the song. A man and a woman duet together, their voices delicately moving around each other in sultry Serbian.

The television presenter says, to the barmaid, one beer please. The barmaid collects a beer from a fridge, opens it and pours it elegantly into a cold glass. The beer looks delicious. The television presenter does not know what beer is. He looks at the beer and doesn't know what delicious is. He is just thinking about his race. He remembers other races that he has had with the other two. He always loses every race. That's the rule.

You always lose every one, because you are known as the slowest out of all of us, the ugly one always says.

The television presenter takes a little beer into his mouth and swills it around.

You have to lose every race, that's your thing, says his agent constantly, you have a good thing going. It's your thing. You have to do your thing. You are good at it. You should be proud of your thing.

Agents and ugly ones and small ones. The presenter feels something like anger. The feeling passes quickly and it is replaced with nothing. He has another sip of his beer and thinks about the void.

* * *

Mandy is in her room. She is looking at herself and imagining the television presenter kissing her neck. She feels repulsed. She desperately wants the television presenter to kiss her. She doesn't understand anything about her desires. She looks at her neck. Perfectly smooth, powdery finish, gleaming cream colour, warm to the touch.

She is worried about having a waxy neck instead of a powdery neck. Not powdery like chalk dust or something, she thinks, but just almost imperceptibly powdery, lightly grained, like soft, matte wood.

Has the television presenter noticed her flirting with him on this trip? Has she flirted with him on this trip? She is not sure whether her behaviour has been normal or flirtatious. She has no idea really what flirtatious behaviour is. She thinks that she just wants to offer herself up to the presenter on a silver platter, with her legs a mile apart and a maniacal smile on her face. And then she will feel disgusting as he has sex with her. She doesn't want to think about his penis or, in fact, any aspect of the sex act.

She flicks on the television. Serbian news. A music video. The film *Terminator* with Serbian dubbing. She watches Arnold Schwarzenegger look at the camera and kill something. She thinks that his chest looks a little like a woman's chest. He has nice nipples, she thinks.

She wonders if anyone actually finds Arnie attractive.

Her television company has given her £50 a day expenses to have a nice time in Serbia, but she doesn't know what to spend the money on. £50 is about 6000 Serbian Dinar. She thinks about spending the money on hotel pornography, almost as a joke for herself. She thinks about seeing the expressions on her colleagues' faces. I bought porn because I felt lonely, she would say. Mandy thinks a lot about what other people think about her. She doesn't know what other people think about her.

It's just so hard to know what to do. Mandy often thinks that.

Mandy has always wanted to be as close as possible to celebrity. She doesn't know why. It just seems to be her programming. Someone, before she was born, made her brain want to hunt down celebrity. She studied 'Media' at university, and was always thrilled to flick through her textbooks and occasionally see images of famous stars, next to serious, academic sounding section headings.

She felt justified in studying the media, because of the serious, academic sounding headings in the book. It is an important thing to study.

It is her first time in Serbia. Belgrade is a pretty city, she thinks. She looks from her window; the street below is full of people, bouncing into one another, greeting and singing and drinking and living an average life all together. Mandy pushes her face against the cold glass of the window and blows breath onto the pane. She likes the feeling of the glass against her face.

Having a sudden thought about something, she pulls away from the glass and looks at herself again in the mirror.

I'm going to sleep with him.

She looks very hard at herself and thinks about her physical attributes. She sends a text message to the presenter. It says, Want a drink?

She receives a reply after about fifteen seconds. The reply says, I am already at the bar. They say I am the slowest, but I am not the slowest at getting to the bar, because I am already here. LOL. What drink shall I get you?

Mandy wants to cry. She leaves her room and heads towards the bar.

She thinks about LOL.

* * *

Your father will be back from Serbia in two more days, says Prudence to Ellen.

Ellen had not asked Prudence when her father would be back from Serbia. Prudence had been acting very strangely ever since finding out about the interview at bid-up TV, thinks Ellen.

I am very excited about my interview, says Prudence, again.

I'm really pleased for you mum.

Ellen thinks about a dying foetus. She receives a text message. It is from the lead singer of the band, The Problem. For fuck's sake, thinks Ellen. It says, I am thinking about you. Prudence shoves a piece of roasted beef onto the plate in front of Ellen. She pours thick gravy over the meat and the potatoes that are already on the plate. Blood from the meat pours into the gravy that lies all over it. Ellen looks again at the text message. She can't remember giving the lead singer of the band her number. She can't remember much about the evening at all.

Another message arrives that says I want to see you again. You are amazing. Ellen thinks this guy is a loser. I had sex with a loser. I am not a virgin any more because of a loser.

BOBBY!!!!!!!!!!!!!!!!!!' says Prudence. She has already called Bobby down to dinner three or four times. Ellen thinks that Bobby is probably looking at pornography on the computer. She finds the thought of her brother masturbating very funny. She thinks about his penis – ha ha. She knows that it is disgusting too, but, who cares, come on it's funny. My little brother, wanking, or 'whacking off' or whatever. Ha ha, she thinks.

BOBBY!! says Prudence. DINNER! she says.

Bobby comes down the stairs and sits at the table. He looks weird, thinks Ellen. His eye twitches a little bit. Did it twitch? thinks Ellen. Is that what masturbation does to boys, she thinks.

Bobby, what have you done all day? says Prudence.

I've been working, says Bobby.

Can I have a look at your work? says Prudence.

Why? says Bobby.

Just want to make sure that you are OK, says Prudence.

Bobby mumbles something under his breath.

Sorry Bobby, I didn't catch that.

I am OK, says Bobby. You can come and look at my work if you want.

The three of them eat their meat and potatoes and gravy. It tastes OK, they all think. The meat is sort of dry, even though there is blood coming out of it. The gravy tastes of salt. The potatoes are soft but meant to be crunchy. Everything is not quite good. There is blood and gravy left on Ellen's plate. She doesn't like the thought of the blood. As she eats, she thinks of a poem.

blood on a white plate
don't think of licking it up
you won't feel better

She thinks about this poem. It is inelegant and has no meaning. She finds it satisfying though. She likes the last line, YOU WON'T FEEL BETTER. She thinks about the line.

Her brother doesn't finish his plate of food.

He looks at Prudence and Ellen and says, Can I be excused? I am full.

Prudence looks at the food left on his plate and says, Didn't you like it? Bobby shakes his head and says something about the food being delicious. He eats one more piece of meat and looks at his mother and faintly smiles. He looks weird, smiling.

OK Bobby, up you go. I'll be up to see your work in a while. Will she go up and look at it, Ellen thinks. She thinks that her mother won't. Yesterday evening, Ellen had come downstairs to get something to drink. She had been quiet, because it was late. She had discovered her mother, bent over the William and Kate commemorative plate, possibly crying. She didn't get a good look, because she had felt weird and had gone back up the stairs. Ellen hates the William and Kate commemorative plate. Every time she passes it she thinks, Fuck the royal wedding. Then she feels excited about swearing in her head.

Her mother makes a noise.

Ellen can't decide whether her mother looks sad or happy. She has no idea. Her mother sort of sits comatose at the table, looking at the mess that the three of them have made.

Mum, are you OK?

I am fine, darling, I am fine. Did you have a nice time at your concert the other night? I forgot to ask.

It was fine, says Ellen.

Another text message appears on her phone. It says: I showed your photo to a model scout I know. She thinks you could be a model. Please text back – I know you think I am a dick, I just want the chance to show you that I am not.

Ellen thinks, Model Scout.

Ellen thinks, you won't feel better.

* * *

In the bar in Belgrade, Mandy is trying to move herself into a position in which, if she wanted to, she could casually touch the body of the television presenter, seemingly by accident, but in a way specifically designed to provoke a response of spontaneous, uncontrollable arousal.

Are you comfortable, sitting like that, says the television presenter.

Mandy laughs and tries to look cool and cute.

Yes. I like to sit like this, Mandy says.

They are both drinking one beer each. They take it in turns to take sips from their glasses and then they look at each other and think about the way each other looks.

Do you love working in television? says the presenter.

It's glamorous, says Mandy, trying to accidentally touch the presenter's leg with her leg. Why isn't his leg there, she thinks to herself.

Let's get to know each other, says the television presenter. What makes you tick?

Ha ha I don't know. No one has ever asked me that before. I am single.

That's surprising, because you are intelligent and pretty, and supportive of people.

Mandy's vagina is desperately searching for some cement or glue, to seal itself with. She feels a sort of free-wheeling terror finally decide to settle over her.

I'm married of course. Got two kids and a wife who I love and I am very proud of her and the kids. Being married and having kids is the thing I am proudest of in life.

She feels the television presenter's knee under the table. She is touching it with her own knee. Mandy is connected to the television presenter by a knee.

The television presenter notices Mandy's knee touching his knee. He thinks about his family and about Mandy's waxy vagina. He thinks about the small one and the ugly one and his agent. He thinks about being young. He thinks about a rose, falling from its stalk and landing on hot brown earth and the petals falling from it and alighting on ants and other creatures and the rose's petals somehow causing feelings of sexual ecstasy in the creatures that they touch.

The television presenter moves his head back, flicking his long silver hair backwards. He looks awkward as he does it. Mandy feels like they should be holding hands or something. She wants to say something that will make the television presenter engage with her.

I am very confused, says Mandy.

Confused? says the presenter.

Yes. I am very confused. Mandy puts her hands together and lays them on the table. The television presenter leans forward and takes hold of Mandy's hands. He looks at her with his sincerest eyes and as he thinks, this is weird, he says, I am confused too.

The ugly one and the small one's voices are heard by Mandy and by the presenter somewhere nearby, coming closer. They look at each other and they move their hands away from each other.

The other two presenters come into the bar, shouting noisily and pointing at things.

* * *

The offices of Bidding.tv take up a small part of a much larger building, in the centre of town. They comprise a smart reception area, a traditional open-plan office area, and a fully functioning television studio. Prudence is sitting in the reception area. She is wearing a smart, grey suit with high-heeled shoes and a black, small bag. The atmosphere feels air-conditioned to her.

Light and airy, the reception area is welcoming to anyone who might spend time in it.

Occasionally Prudence looks at the receptionist, who is wearing a headset. The receptionist sometimes says into the headset, Hello, bidding dot tv! and then she directs the call to the right part of the office.

Prudence hasn't heard the phone ring once. She thinks to herself, are silent phones cool now, and, does it vibrate or is there a light or something.

The receptionist looks at her. She says, Prudence, you can go through now, Mr. Urnton is waiting for you. And then, before Prudence has a chance to stand up, or go through, a man appears in the doorway.

Arnold Urnton, he says, and holds out a hand for Prudence to take.

His hand is pulpy, thinks Prudence. As she takes her hand away, she is left with a feeling of discomfort.

I love grabbing life by the tail Prudence – that's why I didn't want to wait for you to come in. Let's get going.

Arnold Urnton turns around and strikes the heels of his shoes together. He starts moving through the open plan office-space of Bidding.tv. Prudence trots behind, mesmerised. The office staff take a million phone calls each, selling huge quantities of items to customers. There is no sound of any phones ringing, just an avalanche of voices shouting, hello, Bidding.tv – how many would you like?

On the wall is a chart. It says 'Royal Wedding Countdown – 48 days to go,' in big flashing letters. There are pictures of many items of royal wedding memorabilia, William and Kate commemorative plate, William and Kate commemorative tea towel, William and Kate commemorative knit-your-own-royal-wedding book, William and Kate commemorative doll, William and Kate commemorative cutlery set, William and Kate commemorative sex toy, William and Kate commemo-rative teddy bear, William and Kate commemorative ceramic dragon, William and Kate commemorative candle, William and Kate commemorative bible, William and Kate commemorative replica engagement ring, William and Kate commemorative bell, William and Kate commemorative medallion.

Prudence feels depressed. She can feel the feeling that tells her to try and be sick in the toilet, starting to tell her to try and be sick in the toilet. She feels like she is surrounded in perspex.

There is a door in the corner of the sales office that Arnold Urnton is taking her towards. She looks at the backs of his shoes. They are gleaming, except for a small weathered patch on the inside edge of the heel.

He clicks his heels together as he enters the small room.

Make yourself comfortable, Prudence.

On the table is a copy of Prudence's CV.

An impressive CV, Prudence.

Thank you.

You've applied for the Producer's job here at Bidding.tv. What attracted you to the role?

She replies automatically to all of the questions that Arnold Urnton asks her. He asks her questions about her past and why she hasn't worked for such a long time. He asks her questions about her experience as a producer and what 'systems' she has used. He asks her questions about whether she likes to take ownership of a project and he tells her that he has her in mind for a particular project. He tells her that the project she will be in charge of will generate huge revenues for Bidding.tv and will ensure the future of the company during these hard economic times. He asks her about her home life and says, just out of interest, and says that he feels good about her. She asks, is there any reason you feel like you can't hire me? and Arnold says, No, Prudence.

They shake hands and Prudence is reminded of the pulpy, unpleasant texture of his hands. Arnold looks very seriously at Prudence and says, we'll be in touch soon.

Prudence smiles and feels excited and frightened. The back of her throat feels slightly raw. It feels a little fibrous and thickly textured. The air-conditioning, thinks Prudence.

As she leaves the offices of Bidding.tv, Prudence takes her phone out of her bag. She scrolls through the contacts in her address book and clicks on the 'Husband' contact. She clicks on the green phone symbol on screen. She holds her phone up to her ear and waits, as it rings. Her husband doesn't pick up the phone. She rings again. Her husband still does not pick up the phone. Prudence turns her phone to 'silent'.

* * *

Tracy's voice buzzes excitedly in Ellen's ear. Ellen is lying on top of the bedclothes, smiling.

You can be one of the models that starts out naked and then that outrageous stylist dresses them and then by the end of it you have a designer look at high-street prices.

I don't want the stylist to touch me, says Ellen.

I hate that programme, says Tracy.

Ha ha ha, says Ellen.

Is your dad still away? says Tracy.

Yes, but he's back soon. I'm dreading it.

We should go out again before he gets back, go out and have a really good time. If you get in touch with the model agency, you'll probably get loads of money and we'll be able to buy loads of stuff, says Tracy in an excited voice.

Ellen feels like she is almost certainly going to end up getting in touch with the model agency. As she talks more to Tracy on the phone about designer clothes and lingerie and sexy male models, she loads up Google Chrome.

She types in, 'buttocks female model' and looks at the images that come up. She looks at herself in the mirror and drops her trousers and looks at her buttocks. They look similar to some of the buttocks of some of the models in the photographs. She thinks about some of her poems.

What are you doing, you seem distracted? says Tracy.

Nothing. Just thinking that I should get in touch with the model agency. And it's a good excuse for seeing the lead singer again! Ellen definitely doesn't want to see the lead singer again. She thinks about his sperm inside her and then thinks briefly about a diagram of some sperm she remembers from a book she read as a child.

Tracy is a virgin.

She thinks about a diagram of the female reproductive system. Her childhood book of the body had personified a lot of the internal organs, but as far as she remembered, not the female reproductive system. It didn't have a cheeky character in the book.

Do you feel better about taking the pill now?

Ellen had told Tracy that the only reason she hadn't got back in touch sooner with the lead singer was because she felt 'weird' after taking the morning-after pill, and that she wouldn't know how to handle seeing him again.

I guess so. I haven't thought about it much. Ellen feels worried suddenly that her mother might be listening to her phone conversation or somehow recording it.

She stops the conversation with an excuse about something, and opens her journal. She looks at her poems. She looks at some poems she wrote two years ago. She tries to remember what she felt like as she wrote the poems.

She can't remember.

She opens more recent poems and reads them, feeling disconnected from the past. She feels disconnected from the person she was even two days, or two hours, or two minutes ago. She puts the poems back into her drawer and writes a text message on her phone.

hi. how r u? sry for nt getting in touch sooner. lost my fone. modlin snds good. wnt coffee sumtime? x ellen x

She receives a reply almost as soon as her message has gone.

hi, good to hear from you. been thinking a lot about you. i can definitely get you model work. are you free tomorrow? x

Ellen replies, yes x

* * *

LOL says the female dwarf. The words appear above her head in a small speech bubble. She makes a cute laughing noise. She is dancing on the corpse of a defeated enemy, doing the traditional dwarvish step-dance that all females are experts at. She is rotating on the spot. She summons a vanity pet. It is a Wolpertinger, one of the rewards for completing the Brewfest seasonal world-event.

Bobby likes the female dwarf. She is cute, he thinks.

Guild runs are always a lot of fun, Bobby thinks, although sometimes he wishes that his guild were a little more serious about raiding.

LMAO, he says back to the female dwarf. She is a new member of the guild. She used to be in a purely social guild, but decided that she would like to undertake some more serious late game content, so joined Bobby's social/raiding guild.

The other members of the raid are socialising by using emotes and making jokes and summoning vanity pets and transforming into other forms if they have the ability. The tank has had to briefly leave the raid to repair his gear, so there is a bit of down time.

Bobby starts dancing and summons a tabby cat pet. The tabby cat looks funny inside the raid dungeon. It looks out of place. Bobby thinks about the juxtaposition of cute items and dangerous environments. He thinks of a dwarven warrior walking through his school pulling aggro on the teachers and stunning them before using Execute on them all after they hit 20% health. That would finish the teachers off pretty quickly.

The female dwarf whispers to Bobby, where are you from? Bobby feels excited. Manchester, he whispers back.

is it good?

don't know

lol

lol

i'm from Frome, it's really boring

where's Frome?

exactly

LMFAO

haha.

real world = shit

real world = waste of time

real world < wow

real world < piece of shit

how long have you been playing wow?

a couple of years, on and off
me too - since halfway through TBC
i love it
how old are you?
23, how about you
26, says Bobby

The tank returns from the repair mission and the raid continues. Bobby accidentally pulls aggro on a boss and dies. The female dwarf resurrects him. Ty, says Bobby. <3, says the female dwarf.

Bobby tries to emote '/blush' but it does not work. He tries '/swoon' but it does not work. Eventually, he emotes, '/love' whilst targeting the female dwarf. IRL, he blushes.

* * *

A mechanic is checking all three cars over. He is making sure that none of the cars develop a mechanical defect before they are meant to. The television presenter is going to be driving a small-type car. The ugly one is going to be driving a large-type car. The small one is going to be driving the same type of car that he always drives.

That is his thing. He really likes a particular model from a particular car manufacturer. It is very important that they all have their thing. The ugly one's thing is 'Really Manly'.

He makes the catchphrases.

He has the stand-out-from-the-crowd hairstyle.

He wears the cowboy boots.

He leads the way by choosing big-type cars.

The cars are ready. The three presenters sit around a table with Mandy and a man who is wearing very large, professional-effect headphones, and aviator sunglasses. They are having a last-minute production meeting about the race.

The television presenter doesn't know who the man wearing the headphones and sunglasses is. He is something vaguely to do with safety, or something, the presenter thinks.

The headphones man starts talking. He talks about the race plan again. He hammers in the funny idea of the television presenter being out in the lead for the majority of the race, and then having to carry out the final mile at a speed of one mile per hour.

Whenever he says 'one mile per hour', the small one and the ugly one look at each other and snigger, lovingly. Mandy looks at the television presenter once during the production meeting. Her little eyes look very loving and desiring, thinks the part of the presenter's brain that isn't thinking about nothing.

When headphones man stops talking, they each charge their glasses with frothy mineral water and stand up. They all look at each other and they say, here's to another really great race, guys, which will be lost by the slow one.

They slosh their glasses together so that all of their waters spill together. The ugly one says, like the Vikings.

The presenter is too busy looking at Mandy to think about a Viking.

I think Mandy needs help to find out about the world and I can help her, he thinks.

I think Mandy is very tender and naïve and I can help her toughen up and be her mentor, he thinks.

I think Mandy is the only thing that I care about and I will walk away from my life back home, he thinks.

What goes on tour stays on tour, he thinks.

I have no control over anything I do or anything I feel and the idea of control is totally unfathomable to me, he thinks.

Let's rock and roll! the presenter screams as loudly as possible. He stares hungrily and powerfully at Mandy and thinks erotically of her waxy vagina.

The other presenters and the headphones man burst into uncontrollable laughter.

They continue laughing as they walk out of the tent. It is just the television presenter and Mandy, together. He feels very hot and he is heaving from his emotional outburst. He says to

Mandy, Mandy I am not confused. I think you are very tender and naïve and I can help you toughen up and be your mentor.

Mandy looks very worried.

I think you are very special.

Mandy moves forward to the television presenter. She puts her hand on his hip and moves very close to him. She opens and closes her eyes and looks at him. He puts his hand on her hip and then moves it into the small of her back. She makes a small noise.

Let's go somewhere, she whispers.

There are around fifty-five minutes before the start of the race.

Where shall we go? says the presenter.

Let's go to your trailer, says Mandy, breathing heavier than usual.

The television presenter wants to move closer to Mandy. He says, good idea. They move apart, try to clear their heads, both think What Is Happening, move together to the door, make an embarrassed noise together, wait for the other to open the door.

Then they are together in the presenter's trailer.

* * *

Prudence is waiting for Bobby by the door.

What's going on, Bobby? she says. She stands in the doorway with her hands on her hips. She seems to be having trouble keeping her head still.

Nothing, says Bobby.

The school rang.

Bobby doesn't say anything. He doesn't look at his mother's eyes. He looks all around her face and then fixes a stare on a spot a little to her left.

Bobby, talk to me, says Prudence. She is finding it difficult to talk to her son. She feels like she is not having the right emotional reactions to events. She thinks about what the right emotional reaction to these events would be and she can't remember.

Bobby remains silent.

Prudence tries to become angry. She looks at her meek son. A few thin shoots of rain start to whip past Bobby.

He thinks about the in-game weather graphics of World of Warcraft. He thinks about how beautiful it is to see the sunrise or sunset in a zone like the Arathi Highlands. The sun is red rimmed and burns as bright as you can imagine. He thinks about writing a song about the luscious environments of the game.

He thinks about his female dwarf.

Prudence moves forward and tries to hug Bobby. She puts her arms around him. He doesn't react. They stand in the rain together for a moment and then they move inside.

I need to do some work, says Bobby.

* * *

A lady with a haircut is sitting across the room from Ellen. Ellen is thinking about a television programme hosted by Colleen Rooney called *Colleen's Real Women*.

Before she came to the agency, she tried to think about whether or not going to a real model agency would be anything like *Colleen's Real Women*. She prepared herself to be surprised by the experience, or at least try to judge the experience without reference to her preconceptions.

A girl comes into the waiting room. She is very beautiful and has a very commercial face, thinks Ellen. She has a shaved head. What do clippers feel like on the head? What does a razor feel like on the head? The girl sits down and crosses and uncrosses her legs and then crosses them over in the other direction and keeps crossing and uncrossing them. She is chewing some gum. Does she do it to exercise her jaw? Will I have to do jaw exercises, thinks Ellen.

Everywhere Ellen looks is the grey and red logo of the model agency. They have branded the stationery on the table, the table itself, the walls, the clock, the receptionist's uniform.

The shaved head girl is still chewing.

A woman wearing a waterproof white and green bib walks through the waiting room. She has a trolley. On the trolley are a selection of small drinks bottles. Some of the contents are cloudy, some are clear. Ellen has no idea what is inside the drinks bottles. The woman shuffles through another door without looking at anyone in the room, or offering any drinks around. What the fuck, thinks Ellen.

A woman comes through a door and looks at Ellen.

Ellen? she says.

Yes, says Ellen. She feels nothing.

Come through please you are very beautiful.

Ellen goes through into another room with the woman. The woman has a tumbling haircut. It is buoyant and bouncing and tumbling all the way down from her scalp to her breasts and mid-back.

The woman doesn't seem to have a face, just a lot of hair and a smile. The woman smiles at Ellen.

Sit down Ellen. How old are you?

Sixteen. Ellen sits down.

Have you ever done any modelling before?

No.

Do you want to be a model?

Ellen doesn't want to be a model.

Yes.

OK let's do some test shots for our records. Stand up.

Ellen stands up. She is moved by the woman in front of a matte grey screen. There is a strong light pointed at Ellen. She stands still and the woman takes photographs of her on a small camera. The camera looks like a box of cards with a hole in it or something. It doesn't even make a clicking noise as the woman takes the photos. What the fuck, thinks Ellen.

OK great those look great we'll be in touch with you to let you know whether we can take you on. How tall are you?

Five foot eleven.

Well done. We will be in touch soon.

There is a knock at the door and the woman with the trolley of small bottles comes in.

Do you want one Ellen? says the interviewing woman.

The woman with the trolley looks at Ellen and doesn't smile. Ellen thinks, is she making a point of not smiling.

No thanks, says Ellen.

Are you watching your figure? says the interviewer.

I don't know, says Ellen.

The interviewer looks at Ellen and puts her hand over her mouth. She starts laughing and laughing. The space where her face is starts wrinkling up and folding in on itself because of her laughing. She beats her stomach with her hand.

Ellen sort of smiles or something and then, after waiting to no avail for the interviewer to stop laughing for thirty seconds, silently turns and exits the room, and then the agency.

* * *

The television presenter is touching Mandy's tongue with his tongue. The two of them are touching each other's bodies. The television presenter puts his penis on a part of Mandy's body, briefly, by accident.

Whoops, he says.

He puts it inside her vagina and Mandy doesn't like it.

Feels uncomfortable, she thinks.

The television presenter feels weird.

Mandy is thinking about her career. How will this affect my career, she thinks. The presenter wants to move Mandy around so that he can see different parts of her body. He is touching parts of her body in a specific order that he thinks will get Mandy excited.

74

Mandy is touching the television presenter's arm with her arm and she says, that feels really excellent.

Mandy thinks, I am having sex with a celebrity. It is an amazing, life changing experience. Mandy is bored.

The presenter thinks about an odd bird that he saw in the morning and looks at Mandy's bum as his penis moves in and out of her. Mandy has a tattoo of a bird on her bum.

Nice tattoo, says the presenter.

Thanks, says Mandy.

Did it hurt? says the presenter.

No, says Mandy.

It's a bird, says the presenter.

Mandy looks over her shoulder and tries to look lustfully at the television presenter. She thinks, insanely, will it turn him on if I stick one of my nipples near my mouth and lick it?

She awkwardly grabs one of her breasts and moves it up to her mouth and licks her nipple. She says, do you like that?

The presenter looks at Mandy almost licking her nipple and thinks, sexy.

How much does a trailer like this cost, thinks the presenter.

Yes, I like it, the television presenter says.

He clumsily moves Mandy into the kitchen area of the trailer, for some reason. He tries to keep his penis inside her vagina as they move, thinking, it will be sexier if I keep it inside her as I move.

Mandy thinks, why is he bringing me here, is he going to use a whisk on my vagina?

I love having sex in the kitchen, says Mandy.

Yes, says the presenter.

It feels like they are a long way apart from each other, shouting through a strong, loud wind.

The television presenter carries on moving his penis around inside Mandy for five minutes and then pulls it out and ejaculates on the kitchen surface by the sink. He says, oh dear, and then goes to the bathroom to get a wet tissue, and a dry tissue.

By the time he is back in the main area of the trailer, Mandy is fully dressed again. She says, no time for a shower.

That was really great, says the television presenter.

Yes, I really liked it, says Mandy.

I love you, says the presenter.

Mandy doesn't say anything.

I want to leave my wife and family and take you travelling with me around the world, says the presenter.

Mandy doesn't say anything.

The television presenter looks around the trailer at pictures of his family, ornaments from his travels, items of clothing, bits of paperwork. He thinks about the high level of finish on the surfaces of the trailer and tries to think about whether or not the TV company would have paid any more for this deluxe model trailer than an ordinary one.

The door handles are metal. Really swanky, he thinks.

We don't have long to go until the start of the race, says Mandy.

Yeah, says the presenter.

The presenter's consciousness is floating above reality, unable and unwilling to understand or compute or process anything that is happening to it. He doesn't feel as though he exists. It doesn't feel like anything at all.

His actions have no cause and no effect.

* * *

We would like to offer you a job Prudence.

Prudence is shaking with joy. Her eyelashes bounce up and down. She is a hummingbird.

Really?

Yes. I was really impressed with your passion and experience. You have a great personality and seem tenacious and results focussed.

I am, says Prudence the fluttering dragonfly.

And I have some really great news for you. We don't want you to just come in and be a producer. We want you to be a project manager.

Great. That sounds really great.

It's the most important project that we are working on at the moment. The last project manager quit a week ago and we need someone passionate to come in and organise the sales team to try and make the most of a once in a lifetime opportunity.

The phone seems clammy against Prudence's face all of a sudden. Feels like cold flesh. 48 days to go.

Right, says Prudence.

It's the job of managing the Will and Kate countdown sales special.

Yes, says Prudence. She looks at the Will and Kate commemorative plate on her mantelpiece. She thinks, poorly coloured, amateurish finish, passing resemblance at best.

So, what do you think? Do you need some time to think it over? I'll need to know by tomorrow so we can get our second choice if you don't fancy it.

She doesn't need the money. She doesn't need to improve her CV. She has everything she needs at home.

Right. No. I'll take it. Prudence makes herself smile so that her voice sounds happy on the phone. She wraps the cord of the telephone around her finger many times, hoping that the signal will cut out if she wraps it tight enough. She thinks about Kate Middleton's wedding ring.

She thinks about selling a commemorative replica Kate Middleton brand wedding ring to the British and international market. She thinks about lying on the wedding altar and ripping apart her stomach and spraying her intestines and kidneys all over the happy couple and their families. She thinks about wrapping her thick, looping guts around Kate Middleton and William Whatever His Surname Is and squeezing the life out of herself all over them.

She thinks about the blood pouring out of her.

I'm really happy to take this job.

She puts the phone down and sits on a chair. She has a cup of tea. She calls her friend and arranges a lunch date. She wants to tell her friend in person that she is going to be doing her bit for the royal wedding. She wants to tell her friend that she is going to be spreading a little bit of history around the globe. She wants to eat a quail's egg with her friend and talk about her contribution to the history books.

She calls up to Bobby, doing his homework, I got the job, Bobby. No answer comes from upstairs. She thinks about going upstairs and telling Bobby. Bobby doesn't care about my life, she thinks.

She dials the presenter's mobile number. He doesn't pick up.

Ellen is out. Prudence stands up. She can't think of anything to do. She is supposed to be speaking to people, telling them her good news. Prudence feels herself walking around, without really thinking about it. The kitchen would think, this is unusual behaviour from Prudence. She does a lot of circuits of the kitchen. As she walks around the kitchen she thinks about every element of her life. She thinks about her personal history. She thinks, what is the royal wedding of my life.

She can't think of anything.

Later, when Ellen comes home, Prudence will tell her that she got the job. Ellen will seem strangely detached and unexcited. Prudence will almost not notice. Ellen will give her mother a hug and then later tell her brother to say congratulations to his mother. Bobby will forget to say congratulations.

Prudence will not be able to think of anything that was the royal wedding of her life.

Eventually she will think, I love Kate Middleton.

Eventually she will think, Fuck Kate Middleton.

* * *

He rounds a corner. Bits of road surface spray away under the force of his wheels. He rounds another corner. He accelerates, wildly thinking about vaginas and wives, eyes bulging out of his head and silver hair streaming like a unicorn's mane behind him in the hot Serbian wind and feeling on the rim of something he can't understand, something like madness, or the absence of madness and the absence of everything or some rabbit, wild eyed, scratching for sanity in the dark of a warren being filled with cement.

I am the car, he thinks. I am better than these cloud bitches and these car bitches, he thinks. I am better than the trees and the earth under the tree bitches.

What is everything, he thinks.

I am a shit, he thinks. He thinks about a shit in a toilet and thinks that he is like it.

The countryside is going past him fast. He can't make anything out really. I am the car, he thinks. Fuck my children. Am I a father.

He is about ten miles away from the end of the race and he is deciding that fuck it all I am going to win. Huge divots of road surface spray thickly from his spinning wheels. He thinks about spikes coming out from the wheels and him tearing the countryside apart with the spikes.

I AM BOUDICCA.

There is a camera inside the car that normally films pithy monologues about petrol or about the feeling of being stuck to the road. Today it is filming the presenter grinding his teeth together very hard. A voice on a walkie talkie says, ok time to stop the car and develop a problem with your engine.

The television presenter accelerates.

CAN'T SEEM TO STOP he screams at the walkie talkie. THERE IS A PROBLEM WITH THE BRAKES, IT SEEMS!

He is in the last four miles of the race. His heart is being split apart. In the middle of his heart is Mandy's vagina, splitting it apart. There are engines attached to each side of his heart, pulling it apart. Pull the fucking heart apart, he thinks, Prudence, pull it apart, Bobby, Ellen, pull it apart.

You need to stop your car now. Pull over and start fiddling with the engine or we will have to do the whole race again.

The television presenter knows that he doesn't want to fake the end of the race. He wants to try and win it. He doesn't care about the race, he doesn't care about winning. He thinks, definitively and finally that nothing about the race either does or doesn't matter and that his home life might exist and that he is not a part of anything except the decisions that he might be making or that might already be made for him or might not be decisions at all.

I've always wanted to be famous, he thinks.

I've always wanted to have long hair and be young, he thinks.

I've always wanted to drive fast through life and not be the slow one, he thinks.

He turns the walkie talkie off and cruises at huge speed around the remaining Serbian curves and straights. He is travelling, on average, at 85mph.

He sees the finish line. He turns sharply. His car catches on a bit of uneven road surface. It spins through the air and lands smashing into the ground. He won the race.

* * *

In the shade Ellen still wears sunglasses and her phone starts to ring. It is an unknown number.

It's Direct Modelling, says the woman on the phone.

Hi, says Ellen.

You have to come in again because we are going to do a professional quality portfolio for you so that you can get some modelling work. When can you come in? says the woman.

I can come in at the weekend because I have school during the week.

No you have to get time off school we will call the school you are going to be the next Lily Cole, says the woman.

Who is Lily Cole? says Ellen.

The woman on the other end of the phone snorts out a piggy little laugh.

The great thing about you is that you have a personality, Ellie.

I don't really like being called Ellie, I prefer Ellen.

Ellie is cuter that's what we are putting on your portfolio it's no big deal just a better way for people to remember you, it rhymes with Lily. We'll speak to your teacher and get you some time off so that you can come and do your portfolio. Let's say first thing Monday, come to the offices and you are a very lucky girl.

Ellen hangs up the phone and feels weird. She thinks about Tracy. She sends a text message to Tracy telling her that she got the modelling job, she thinks. Almost immediately, Tracy sends a text back saying, u r gorgeous, of course they want u x x x

Ellen masturbates. She is sort of crying.

* * *

Bobby always used to get nervous in the newsagent, waiting to buy his pornographic magazines. He doesn't any more. He has learned that the man behind the counter needs his money just as much as Bobby needs the magazines. He must think that it doesn't do young lads any harm to masturbate to pornographic images. Why would it do any harm? It's only natural, he must think.

Bobby reaches for the top shelf and takes down one porn magazine. There are black circles covering the nipples of the lady on the front cover. She is wearing polka-dot knickers. The magazine costs £4.95. If he sells each page with an image on it that is not totally dominated by adverts he will make enough for two months of World of Warcraft.

Luckily, he doesn't have to buy any more expansion sets for a while, so his expenditure shouldn't be that high over the next few months. He shouldn't have to save up like he had to for his first month's subscription.

The man behind the counter is not the usual man behind the counter. He is an older guy. Grey hair, cardigan, drooling maybe. Has very thin rimmed spectacles.

Looks like a tall gnome, thinks Bobby.

The tall gnome coughs a lot and makes the noise of phlegm being brought up into the mouth. He swallows his phlegm. Bobby thinks, disgusting.

Hello I want this please, says Bobby.

Not old enough, says the old man.

I am old enough.

How old are you?

Eighteen.

That's not old enough.

It is old enough. That's the law. I am old enough.

If that's the law and you really are eighteen then go and get a policeman and get him to arrest me for not obeying the law, says the old man. He crosses his arms and looks very happy with himself.

Bobby imagines the old man filling in old fashioned logic puzzles in books that existed before the days of sudoku.

Look. I am not eighteen, OK. But I need that magazine. I will pay extra.

Please stop trying to buy this magazine. Just buy FHM or something.

I don't want fucking FHM you stupid cunt, says Bobby.

He throws the magazine on the ground and steps on it. The old man looks scared.

You are a fucking idiot, says Bobby.

Bobby thinks about not being able to play World of Warcraft and he becomes angry. He throws over a stack of magazines. He opens a freezer and throws the ice-creams from inside onto the floor and steps on them. He throws chocolate bars from the counter onto the tall gnome. He shouts, tall gnome! at the tall gnome.

He turns and walks out of the newsagent. On his way out he tries to slam the door, but an automatic dampening mechanism makes it silently and gently close. Bobby doesn't really understand why he did any of the things that he did inside the newsagent, or before coming to the newsagent, or anything he has ever done in his life.

Outside, in the rain, Bobby thinks about other newsagents in the area. There are not any. He needs to make money soon, or his subscription will run out. He will miss out on raids and he will not be able to see the female dwarf. He will have to think up a very clever excuse for the female dwarf if his subscription runs out. He will have to tell her that he went on a business course or that he went to an international poker tournament or something else sexy. What is sexy, he thinks.

Fuck pornography, he thinks.

As he runs home he tries desperately to think of other money making opportunities. He thinks that maybe his father will pay for his subscription if his grades improve or if his teachers say nice things. But he doesn't have time. There must be another way. Is there stuff in the house that his mother wouldn't miss if he sold it? Nothing expensive, just things that his school friends would want. When is his dad getting back from Serbia? What would his dad pay for? A football club or something? His dad paid for so much crap that Bobby didn't want, why wouldn't he pay for the one thing that he did want?

Approaching his drive, he sees his mother and his sister outside the house. His sister is in her school uniform, she must have just arrived home. His mother is wearing an apron. He can't smell dinner. They are hugging each other. They both look distraught. What is the problem? Bobby hopes that whatever they are upset about won't stop him from playing World of Warcraft this evening. He has commitments.

He is close now and his mother has seen him. She moves towards him, crying heavily.

Bobby, your father has had an accident.

Bobby looks at his sister who stands, slump-shouldered by the front door.

He doesn't feel anything.

A white space inside him just wants to be in Azeroth.

Part Three

The doctor flutters around the room, his clipboard fanning the patients in the ward. The presenter looks at the doctor. His eyes are open just a little. He is in pain. The pain is coming from his legs and his head. The doctor comes over and makes some little movements next to him. The television presenter is not sure what he is doing. Seems to be adjusting something.

He tries to think, my pain is nothing. He finds it difficult to convince himself that his pain is nothing. How can my pain be something when I am nothing, he thinks. Did I win the race, he thinks. He imagines watching the footage of the crash back with the ugly one and the small one.

He imagines the small one rewinding and playing the footage over and over again. Look at your face, the small one says in his imagination. In his imagination his face seems ridiculous. It looks like someone else's face. He has never seen his face making this expression in the mirror.

Are you in pain? says the doctor.

Yes, says the presenter.

This button controls how much painkiller you get. You press it more to get more painkiller. Do you understand?

Yes.

Don't worry, you can't overdose, it's been calibrated to be safe for your body mass.

Right.

Have as little as you can manage. It is not good for you.

OK.

The doctor moves from one wall to the other. He lifts his legs up very high as he walks. He seems to do twirling movements with his hands as he walks. His walk is sarcastic. The presenter's head hurts more. His family are coming to visit him later on. He doesn't remember when visiting hours are.

The presenter presses for more painkillers. He presses the button for a long time.

The world is a little bit further away from him. His thoughts are the thoughts of someone else. He doesn't have to worry about thinking them, they just happen, it seems. He moves his eyes left and right a little bit and feels something. He doesn't know what he is feeling. It's a response to something that he hasn't perceived. A beautiful bird or a phoenix, roasting a fire in front of him. All of his memories are here, the things that make him. What can he do to keep them together, wheat tied by a string at the centre, it makes him. Wheat tied by a string at the centre he starts to sing.

> Wheat, tied by a string at the centre,
> My poor heart is wheat tied in two,
> Sweet, the girl burning bright in the centre,
> The girl that I love is you girl,
> The girl that I love is you.

He sings his tune and words sweetly, pushing it out onto the world around him. Prudence, the love of his life is floating in front of him, surrounded by Bobby and Ellen, fragments of himself, his connection to the future, the line that ties the wheat of his past to whatever may happen to humanity in hundreds and thousands of years. They are the unbroken line of sentient matter that derives from the first movements of the universe. They both came from a penis that came out of another penis that came out of another penis that came out of another penis that came out of another penis that came out of another penis that came out of another penis that came out of another penis that came out of another penis that came out of another penis that came out of another penis that came out of another penis that came out of another penis that came out of another penis

that came out of another penis that came out of another penis
that came out of another penis that came out of another penis
that came out of another penis that came out of another penis
that came out of another penis that came out of another penis
that came out of another penis that came out of another penis
that came out of another penis that came out of another penis
that came out of another penis that came out of another penis
that came out of another penis that came out of another penis
that came out of another penis that came out of another penis
that came out of another penis that came out of another penis
that came out of another penis that came out of another penis
that came out of another penis that came out of another penis
that came out of another penis that came out of another penis
that came out of another penis that came out of another penis
that came out of another penis that came out of another penis
that came out of another penis that came out of another penis
that came out of another penis that came out of another penis
that came out of another penis that came out of another penis
that came out of another penis that came out of another penis
that came out of another penis that came out of another penis
that came out of another penis that came out of another penis
that came out of another penis that came out of another penis
that came out of another penis that came out of another penis
that came out of another penis that came out of another penis
that came out of another penis that came out of another penis
that came out of another penis that came out of another penis
that came out of another penis that came out of another penis
that came out of another penis that came out of another penis
that came out of another penis that came out of another penis
that came out of another penis that came out of another penis
that came out of another penis that came out of another penis
that came out of another penis that came out of another penis
that came out of another penis that came out of another penis
that came out of another penis that came out of another penis
that came out of another penis that came out of another penis

that came out of another penis that came out of another penis
that came out of another penis that came out of another penis
that came out of another penis that came out of another penis
that came out of another penis that came out of another penis
that came out of another penis that came out of another penis
that came out of another penis that came out of another penis
that came out of another penis that came out of another penis
that came out of another penis that was the first penis.

When they hug him he is hugging the future and the past.
They are talking to him and his brain automatically selects the
perfect reply to every question that they ask. He talks passionately
to them about his love and about his worry in the last moments
of the crash being that he may never see them again. Beautiful
Ellen and proud Bobby cry together, not knowing what to feel,
but the presenter, lying on the bed, knows exactly what to feel
because he doesn't think about it, he feels it by accident, with
no thought, just existence, making his decisions for him.

* * *

Bobby is walking up the slope at school, toward the block where
the modern languages lessons are held. He is thinking, World
of Warcraft.

He sees people who he recognises and who nod at him as
he passes. He doesn't nod. He keeps his eyes forward. He is
thinking about his feet crunching into the snow in Dun Morogh.
People know that his father is in hospital. They don't know what
to say to him.

Sometimes Bobby wonders why everything he sees is not
clickable. He thinks, should I right-click or left-click this object
to interact with it?

In his bag are some of the books he needs for his lessons. He
has forgotten to bring the books he needs for French, which is his
next class. Normally, if you forget your textbook for French, you
get worried. The teacher, Mr. Florette, is a hard-nut. He once,
some students say, grabbed hold of a student and threatened to

shake him. He once told a student to look out of the window for a whole lesson, wearing a sign that said 'idiot'. He once made an entire classroom of students cry, some students say.

No one really knows which of the stories about Mr. Florette are real.

The profession trainers in World of Warcraft are much less frightening than Mr. Florette. They don't tell you off for forgetting your books, or going to the wrong lesson. They just calmly and instantly teach you everything that you need to know. No hassle, no threats.

One of Bobby's friends sees him and comes up to him and walks with him up the hill to the French classroom. He talks to Bobby for the five minutes it takes to get to the room. Bobby doesn't listen to anything he says. He is vaguely aware of his friend, and the things he says to him. It feels like the actions of the two of them are going on somewhere else, somewhere totally unrelated to the world that Bobby's brain is floating through, totally unrelated to Azeroth, and Earth.

Just as Bobby and his friend reach the modern languages block, it begins to rain and the ground starts to smell. Bobby is aware of the smell of the earth for less than a second, and then he is inside.

The students take their books out of their bags and put them on the desks in front of them. Mr. Florette sits at the head of the classroom. His moustache is the main indicator of his mood. His eyes don't move.

He says, Le subjonctif. Ouvrez vos livres.

The students open their books. Mr. Florette's moustache seems calm. Because Bobby doesn't have his book, he shares with Alex Grantham, who he sits with. Alex Grantham is an average guy with a French book.

For the first five minutes of the class, Mr. Florette doesn't notice that Bobby doesn't have a book. He stays at the front of the room, calmly speaking to the students through his moustache.

And then, he tells the students to do an exercise.

Pas de travail ensemble! he says.

The students all turn to their own copies of their books, and their own private exercise books. Bobby just sits there, looking straight ahead into a display on the wall. The display is about the French revolution. It is silent in the classroom.

Mr. Florette is looking at Bobby. His moustache is moving.

Bobby Martin, he says.

Bobby doesn't say anything.

Where is your textbook?

Bobby doesn't say anything. He is looking at a picture of a decapitated head. He hasn't processed the image into a piece of data. It remains just a collection of colours arranged in particular shapes.

Mr. Florette stands up, and walks between the desks to reach Bobby's. He looks at the surface of the desk and sees that there is only one textbook. Bobby is still looking straight ahead. Things seem to be happening around him to do with a teacher, or something.

Bobby Martin, look at me when I am talking to you, says Mr. Florette, calmly. His moustache is arched in a very stern way.

Bobby continues to stare forward, at the splashes of colour that make up the shape of the head, and the bright background.

Bobby? Can you hear me? Mr. Florette clicks his fingers sharply in front of Bobby.

Nothing happens.

The rest of the class start to quietly laugh and talk to each other. Mr. Florette looks around at the class and they stop talking.

Bobby Martin. Answer me right now. He lowers his head a little so that he is at eye level with Bobby. He looks straight at him.

There is a knock at the door. Mr. Florette looks away from Bobby and walks to the door. He opens it a little and has a quiet discussion with someone outside. The students keep their heads forward. They can only hear whispers.

Mr. Florette walks up to Bobby. He moves his head down to Bobby's ear. Bobby, go with the headmaster, he says.

Bobby turns to the door and sees the headmaster through the open gap. His eyes are bubbling with anger.

* * *

Prudence is by the presenter's side. They are talking about her new job.

I am proud of you, says the presenter.

I love you, says Prudence.

They carry on talking. The presenter says that he is feeling better. He says that Prudence absolutely must go to her job, she doesn't have to come and visit him. She says that they were OK with her coming in tomorrow instead of today. She tells him that she is the project manager for the Will and Kate wedding campaign. She tells him about the products that she has to sell. They both laugh about the commemorative products and feel young and close to each other.

Every hour or so, the presenter presses the button that gives him more painkiller.

* * *

She is a little bit too close to another woman wearing not many clothes. Ellen doesn't like it. She doesn't care. She thinks about being this close to Tracy with no clothes on. She thinks about the way Tracy smells, when they are close. Ellen is getting paid one thousand pounds for these photographs.

When they have finished she sits down on a chair with something wrapped around her bare shoulders. It's a fur wrap. She has bare feet with cute nail polish on them. She has bare legs with shimmering powder on them. She is wearing hot pants that are made of plastic. She is wearing weird circles made of plastic over her breasts. She is wearing make up. All of the things touching her body fuck her.

She sends a text message to her mother that says, OMG I am a model. How is dad? She sends a text message to Tracy that says, not as glamorous as I thought... She sends a text message to the lead singer that says, bored, wish you were here.

She thinks about trying to make the three text messages into a poem.

not glamorous
bored wish you were here
fuck my life
fuck my life
fuck my life
how is dad?

Someone shows her a piece of clothing and Ellen says, that is cute. She wants to be at home and feels like crying. She wants to be in her room and be reminded of her childhood. Childhood is nothing, she thinks. Adulthood is nothing, she thinks.

Dad is fine, says the first text.

Thinking about you sexy, says the second text.

I am so jealous, says the third text.

There is a quiet storm going on behind her eyes. She thinks about who sent her each text message and about the relationship that generated the text messages. She thinks about Tracy and about the lead singer.

She types in, I want to see you naked. She feels aroused and feels tender. She finds Tracy's number in her phone. No-one in the world is happy. Behind all happiness is sadness. The sadness of being aware of being alive. The sadness of knowing that although you have the power to do whatever you like, you never will. The sadness that comes from mortality, and from self-awareness. The sadness that comes from knowing what kind of a piece of shit you really are, and never being able to show anyone what sort of a piece of shit you are. The sadness of never knowing what to do, and having to pretend that you know what you are doing. The sadness of time. The sadness of enjoying misery and wanting to dip further and further into it, until every breath that you take is colourless and cold.

Ellen presses send. She waits.

All she wants is for Tracy to reply to her saying that their lives are one and that she wants to see her naked and that they are meant to be together. All she wants is for someone else to feel something the same as her.

She sits in her chair, wrapped in fur and surrounded by people fussing over each other and the set and the costumes. A woman carrying a tray of something walks around. Can this really be happening, she thinks.

The manager of the shoot is wearing sunglasses, a sock on his penis and some leaves around his shoulders. He is the most fashionable. He tells the models what to do. He tells Ellen that they need to do some more shots of her upper body and of her legs by themselves as the clients may want that or something. Ellen does not listen very closely. She is not interested in anything except her phone, which has not yet beeped.

She gets up and gets posed and gets asked to sit down again. There is still nothing on her phone.

She keeps thinking that her heart is going to stop. It makes her panic. She feels like she is aware of an irregular heart-beat happening.

In another break she picks up her phone and types in, holy shit I am sorry sorry - meant for the lead singer – so gross, forgive me x x so embarrassed.

She receives a reply straight away. The reply says, hahahaha fail.

A man moves in front of her and does some make-up work on her eyes. He accidentally puts a brush in her eye and Ellen shouts, you fucking idiot.

* * *

They all look like normal guys with average lives, thinks Prudence. There is no glamour in this place. There is nothing to even show that it is a TV channel. It's just a bank of sales people, a chart with numbers on, and a lot of morose looking, cheery sounding young guys.

They are called things like Colin and Mandy and Malcolm and Ian and Sharon.

OK team it's lovely to meet you all properly. We will get to know each other over the next few weeks. I am good at motivating people so get ready for your figures to improve and I know the TV business inside out so get ready for ratings to soar. I am passionate about the royal wedding. We are helping as many people as possible to buy their little part of history. That's the catchphrase I want you to build into your sales patter. I want you to say "It's your chance to be a little part of history". No-one wants to miss this event, everyone wants to be able to say where they were when the royal wedding happened, and what commemorative items they had bought that were on display on the big day.

We're living for that day, guys. For that big day when we are part of history. In my life, I've learned that you've got to love the things that go on around you. Things like the royal wedding. It's heaven. It's heaven on earth, guys.

The sales staff look like they are confused by Prudence's motivational speech. Arnold Urnton watches at the side of the room, waiting for his new hiring to do something inspirational, or target driven.

Prudence doesn't know what to do. She feels like she has finished her speech. Is she meant to tell them to get on the phone? She thinks about her husband, lying in a hospital bed, feeling proud of her. Why are you proud of me, she thinks. She wonders if he is thinking of her.

What is the royal wedding of my life, she thinks.

She feels happy that she seems to be able to talk and connect to the presenter recently. Since he came back from Serbia he seems closer to me, she thinks. All it took was for him to nearly die, she thinks.

All it takes for someone to feel fine is to nearly die, she thinks. Come and kill me, salespeople, she thinks.

The salespeople continue to sit in front of her, unmotivated, chewing gum, looking vacant.

Do it for Kate and Wills, she says.

* * *

It is a cold day. It's raining. There are the sounds of rain all around. There is the smell of the cold and the rain. There are leaves of trees being moved by rain and by wind. There are puddles of water that car tyres move through. There are cyclists, wet through, with seeping bottoms, heads and legs. There is the taste of rain in the air.

The television presenter gets out of the passenger side of the car. He is home. Parts of his body are still recovering. He has crutches to help him walk. He can't be bothered to talk. The effects of the painkillers from the hospital are wearing off. His body is starting to hurt again.

Prudence gets out of the car. She is standing in the rain. She looks like she is determined to try and not look upset.

Come on love, she says.

She walks round the car in the rain and helps the presenter to move away from the car and into the house.

He sits in the living room and looks out of the window. The painkillers have completely worn off after another thirty minutes.

Prudence sits in the kitchen, looking through at the presenter looking out of the window.

He thinks about nothing.

He looks at the trees and the water and the rain and feels nothing. In an hour, Bobby comes home from school. He is in trouble for smashing up a newsagents. The presenter doesn't speak to him. He hears Prudence say a few words to Bobby.

Ellen comes home from a fashion shoot. She seems miserable. The presenter doesn't say anything to Ellen. Prudence has put up a poster on the wall. It is a countdown to the royal wedding. She has put her commemorative plate in a prominent place on the wall. The presenter doesn't say anything to Prudence.

It's dinner. There is a meal on the plate in front of the presenter. He eats mouthfuls of the meal without tasting or noticing the food. He gets a message on his phone from the ugly one and the short one saying get better soon you wuss. He doesn't reply to them. He thinks about not getting a message from Mandy. He thinks about not hearing from Mandy since they had sex. Did we have sex, he thinks. " " he thinks.

He sighs without making a noise.

Bobby what are we going to do about you. Why are you buying pornography? Why are you smashing up newsagents? says Prudence.

Bobby doesn't say anything.

How is your modelling? I am worried about your school work, Ellen.

Ellen doesn't say anything.

What's the matter, guys? she says.

TALK TO ME! Prudence screams.

* * *

Bobby is suspended from school for two days. The man from the newsagents had been in the school office. He and the teachers had asked Bobby many questions about why he had done what he had done.

The man from the newsagents had said, yes, that's him.

Then he left.

Then the annoying questions and attempts to help began.

A teacher said, why were you trying to buy pornographic magazines? Bobby had thought at the time, just call it porn.

Are you having problems with a girl? they had asked.

You are lucky we haven't got the police involved, they had said.

You committed a crime, they said.

Masturbation is a normal part of growing up, they said.

Do you think this behaviour is acceptable, they said.

Bobby had not answered any questions. He just sat there and took it all unflinchingly. He had just thought about that evening's raid in World of Warcraft. He thought about how important it is to make sure that all of his tactics were correct. He thought that he hoped that his guild-mates didn't ask him to tank this evening. He found tanking stressful.

The teacher had asked something about Bobby needing counselling. Bobby decided that it was important to try and stop them saying things to him.

I am just really upset at the moment because my dad was in hospital and I thought he was going to die. I am really sorry. I think I am stressed.

Bobby hears occasionally that a lot of people blame a lot of things on stress.

We know it's a hard time for you Bobby, and that's why we are being lenient. We are not going to exclude you, we are just going to suspend you for a couple of days.

Bobby was very happy. Two days to play World of Warcraft.

But I need you to know just how serious this is, Bobby. There will come a point in your life when you will have to start taking responsibility for your actions. Everyone has difficult things to deal with, that's life. If I were to go into a newsagents and do what you did and then said it was because my wife had just died or whatever, I would still get tried in a criminal court. Do you understand, Bobby? A criminal court.

Two days of World of Warcraft sounds fine.

* * *

Ellen is having sex with a photographer. He is a little bit handsome and wanted to have sex with her so she decided that it was OK. There is some music playing in the background. He sounds like an animal. He is wearing sunglasses. After he ejaculates and throws the tied up condom in the bin he takes his sunglasses off and winks at her.

You are so beautiful, he says.

She is lying on the bed. She hasn't moved since he had sex with her. She says, thanks.

Do you want a cigarette? he says.

Sure, she says.

So do you have a boyfriend? he says.

I have someone who thinks he's my boyfriend, she says.

She thinks about sitting on the wall in school with Tracy, swinging their legs in the wind and eating tuna sandwiches. She hasn't seen much of Tracy since her modelling started taking up more of her time.

Someone at the agency had convinced the school that it was too good an opportunity for her to miss, and they had agreed to some home schooling so that her grades weren't impacted that much.

Do you want to have sex again, says Ellen. She still hasn't moved. She is smoking the cigarette and tapping the ash onto her stomach.

Baby you're so sexy, says the photographer. It's transgressive what you are doing. It's like, is this self-harm? Is this addiction? Is this what the youth are doing to themselves to get a bigger kick? He takes a photograph of Ellen tapping ash onto her stomach. He keeps saying how sexy it is, how young and beautiful she looks, how hot and sexy this situation is, and how many boundaries and taboos are being shattered. He works himself up into a state of arousal as he takes more photographs of Ellen's stomach.

What's the career path that a model normally takes, says Ellen.

Haha, says the photographer. You have a personality, Ellie. That's why you are such a good model.

Ellen says, No I mean it, what happens after you do Modelling. What's the point after that, what do you do?

No one knows, baby. No one knows what they are going to be doing after they finish doing whatever they are doing. You just have to react to the situation!

You are a fucking moron, thinks Ellen. What am I doing to myself? thinks Ellen. Am I doing all of this for love? thinks Ellen.

She says, I'm going.

You don't want to have sex again?

No. I'm going. You're an idiot.

What the fuck?

You're a fucking idiot.

She gets up, wipes the ash off her stomach, puts clothes on quickly and then runs to the bus stop. She shows the bus driver her young person's bus pass. She sits at the back of the bus, thinking that she should cry, unable to feel anything.

I think that I only will ever love Tracy, she thinks. I think that I will only never love anyone, she thinks. I think I wish I was pregnant so that I knew what to do in life, she thinks. I think I just want to try and write poems again and not take any drugs and not be a model, she thinks.

A text message arrives.

It is from the photographer. It says, I want to see you again, I can get us tickets to a private party with the stylist from that naked programme do you want to come.

She replies: get 3 tickets and I will come. One for my friend.

He replies: sure, see you soon sexy x x x

She sends a message to Tracy: miss you. got us tickets to a private party with our favourite tv stylist. should be funny. we can take the piss out of him. let's do it — really miss you x

Ellen waits for the reply. When it comes, it says, SO EXCITING X X X X XX X

* * *

He gets on the bus because he can't drive. He walks from the bus stop to the doctors using his crutches. He doesn't notice anyone. He thinks " ".

The receptionist asks him his name and he tells her. She asks him to sit and he does. A woman next to him coughs and he looks round. The room has a smell and he notices it. The receptionist calls his name and he stands. His brain tells him to move and he does.

The doctor talks to him about pain management without really looking at him. He mumbles about pain being manageable using strong willpower, effectively not allowing yourself to feel pain.

The presenter thinks, give me strong painkillers.

The doctor looks over from his computer and has a good look at the presenter. He says, It's you from that television show, isn't it. The car show, what's it called.

That's right, says the presenter.

I had no idea I'd be treating a celebrity today! I love your show. What's he like, the ugly one?

Who knows? says the presenter.

HAHAHAHA, says the doctor, laughing.

I could hit him with my crutch and then take the painkillers, thinks the presenter. I'm stupid, thinks the presenter.

Is that how you got into your accident? On the show, with a supercar?

Yes.

Oh wow! I won't tell anyone, I'll keep it to myself. Do you want a general check-up while you're here? Take your blood-pressure, check your urine, anything like that?

No, I'll be OK. Just something for the pain, I think.

No problem at all. You just have to remember not to take these for more than three days in a row. They can be habit forming.

Yeah. I'll just use them when the pain is unbearable.

The pain is always unbearable. He doesn't know what pain is, and that is why he can't bear it.

That's right. I'll give you the really strong ones as well. They will knock you out a bit, but the pain should completely disappear. Don't drive when you take them. Don't use any heavy machinery. Hahaha. Don't blow up any caravans.

Am I meant to laugh, he thinks. He thinks that he is meant to at least smile. By the time the thought has been processed, the time to smile has gone. What do I do now that I missed the right moment to smile, he thinks. What does a tree do when it forgets to shed its leaves in the autumn, he thinks. What does a glass do when it hits the ground and forgets to smash?

The doctor looks a little bit confused. Perhaps the doctor thinks that he did something wrong in the conversation. Maybe it's not just me, thinks the presenter. There is no such thing as just me, he thinks.

The doctor prints a prescription and hands it to the presenter. How's the pain now? he says.

Bad, says the presenter.

Here, take these.

The doctor takes a blister pack of pills out of his drawer and pops two out. He hands the presenter the pills and gives him a glass of water.

The most important thing to do is rest. Give your body time to mend. You won't be able to work for a while, so you might as well be comfortable.

The presenter puts the pills on his tongue. Feels chalky, he thinks. He swallows the pills with a mouthful of water.

Thirty minutes later, on the bus, the clouds are ripped apart and replaced with the mellow afternoon light of a childhood summer's day. The presenter breathes and loves the world. He feels the pack of pills in his pocket and thinks that he is alive.

* * *

Bobby is alone at home with his dad. His sister is doing modelling. His mother is at work. Dad has been weird since coming back from the doctor's, thinks Bobby. He walks over to the door and locks it. He is going to work on his professions in the morning, do a few heroics in the afternoon and then join in with a guild raid in the evening. Tomorrow will be the same, and then back to school.

He sits down at the computer and waits for it to start. He is thinking about the Tier 11 pieces that he is still missing. He is thinking about which bosses drop the gear. One of the bosses is optional so he will have to ask his group to go out of their way to do him. But that is OK, because in World of Warcraft people like him. He has friends, who talk to him about life and their shared interests. People who will go out of their way to help him. People don't judge him by who his father is or how much of a failure he is or how fat or thin or bad at school and rugby he is. The female dwarf even whispers to him in the game and that is a private conversation between the two of them because she wants to speak to just him and no-one else because he is funny and intelligent.

Before logging on he goes to www.wow.joystiq.com and reads the day's articles on the game. He downloads a World of Warcraft podcast to listen to while he plays. It's easy to keep abreast of the news in the game if you know where to look. Bobby knows where to look.

He double clicks on the World of Warcraft client software and the launcher opens. A small newsfeed runs down the right hand side of the launcher. There is a new expansion set for the World of Warcraft trading card game out this week. Bobby doesn't have anyone to play the game with in real life, so he has never bought the cards, although he has thought about it, because occasionally a card will have an in-game reward.

He clicks the large button in the lower right-hand corner, labelled 'PLAY'. The computer plays an echoing sound effect and the game launches.

He cracks his knuckles.

He types his username and password into the appropriate boxes on the login page. He clicks login. After a brief wait a dialogue box appears on screen. The dialogue box says, This account has no remaining pre-paid game time available. Please visit www.wow-europe.com to update your account.

Bobby presses cancel and types in his login details again. This must be a mistake. The month of play time can't have run out already.

The same dialogue box pops out on screen. Bobby doesn't know what to do. He needs debit card details or he needs a pre-paid game card. He begins to sweat. He sits in his chair sweating and looking at the screen. His body starts to ache. His head starts to ache. He doesn't know what he is feeling. He is out of control of his body.

Outside his window a bird in a nest makes a noise.

Bobby says, shut the fuck up.

I miss you Azeroth, he thinks.

Need fucking money bitches, he thinks.

* * *

We are doing lunch, thinks Prudence. She is eating a piece of cured ostrich skin and a stick from a special edible African tree. Her friend is eating a live fish.

I found out he is having an affair, she says.

Oh no, says Prudence.

Don't care, thinks Prudence.

He has been having sex with someone at work. It's dreadful. It's really the worst thing that has ever happened to me.

Yes it's really bad, says Prudence.

The two of them sit in silence for a minute, eating their food. They both think about filling up the silence, but neither knows how to do it without making the other think, she is just filling up the silence.

My job is going well, says Prudence.

Oh that's fantastic, I'm so jealous, it's wonderful to have a new lease of life so late in!

Right, thinks Prudence.

It's so great to see the new generation of the royal family coming through, isn't it, says Prudence. It's important for us to have role models to look up to, and it's just fantastic that they live such healthy, wholesome lives and they are clever and brave. I mean he is in the army which is just great or the coast-guard, it's just the classic British thing, isn't it, street parties and God save the queen and all that, says Prudence, going berserk.

Oh yes cucumber sandwiches and all that, says her friend.

They should rule us, says Prudence. They should make the laws and they should be back in charge properly. We don't need a constitutional monarchy, I want them to have absolute power. They should be allowed to kill bad people and have whatever they want and do everything they want.

Yes, I agree. We are getting divorced. I am going to take all of his money.

Quite right, says Prudence. She laughs, for some reason. Almost as the laugh leaves her throat she thinks, I am going mad.

So what's it like being the new girl at the office again? says the friend.

It's a real challenge and I am relishing it, says Prudence. She rolls the r sound at the start of the word 'relishing'. Some of her spit flies onto her friend's still-alive fish. It's dying on her plate as she takes more and more bites out of it. The waiter told her to eat one half of it first and then the other half. The half-filleted fish occasionally jerks in agony on the plate. It doesn't seem to have any blood.

It's amazing, you can feel it moving in your mouth, her friend says, swallowing. It's the freshest fish I've ever eaten. They inject it with a solution that flavours it and also dulls its pain so it's humane. It just tastes so strongly of the sea.

Prudence doesn't know what to say or think.

She is stuck looking at the fish on her friend's plate.

Do you want to try some?

No thanks, says Prudence. She thinks, fuck everything that exists.

Go on, try some.

Prudence opens her mouth as if to say something but can't think of anything to say. She sits there with her mouth open.

Come on.

Her friend uses her knife to flip the fish over so that the uneaten side faces up. She puts the knife into the flesh and smoothly cuts a mouth-sized piece.

Is the flesh dead when it's disconnected from the other flesh, thinks Prudence.

Her friend lifts the piece up to Prudence's mouth and puts the mouthful inside. It tastes like the sea. Fuck Kate Middleton, thinks Prudence. Fuck Prince William. Is this the 'royal wedding' moment of my life?

Everyone's life has a royal wedding moment. Make every moment of your life your royal wedding moment. Buy a commemorative royal wedding plate and put it on your wall.

Go to the toilet and try and be sick and think I am nothing forever.

* * *

The front door of the house is open when Ellen gets back from the day's work. That's unusual.

She is tired. She closes the door after her. She wants to watch a lot of YouTube clips of the celebrity stylist so that she can learn about him so that when she meets him she can say things to him about his life.

She puts her bag on the hook in the hallway and pushes the door to the living room open. Her father is sleeping in a chair by the window. There is paper on the floor. Cupboards are open, some ornaments lie on the floor. Pots where money is sometimes kept are emptied.

Have we been robbed, she thinks. She walks over to her father and says, dad wake up. She touches her father's face and he half opens his eyes and doesn't say anything to her. Dad, are you ok, she says. She feels like she is supposed to be worried. She is thinking about stylist videos. I hope we have enough money to let me still go to the party, she thinks. I hope I can kiss Tracy at the party, she thinks.

She shakes her father's shoulder and he wakes a little. She says to him, I think we have been robbed. Her father says, robbers need money for food and drugs.

Dad is weird, she thinks. She looks around the room more and sees that nothing expensive has been taken. It looks like someone who knows the secret places that the family keeps money in has frantically searched the house. I hope that whoever it was hasn't taken my secret money from my room, she thinks.

In her room things are messy. Her drawers are open. Someone has moved her book of poems and her diary. Someone has accidentally knocked over her lava lamp. Ellen tries to cry about her childhood artefacts being destroyed, but can't manage it. Her secret money is gone from inside her drawer.

Her bottle of whisky is still safe in her wardrobe.

She looks in her parents' room. It has been ransacked. She looks at the spare room. The one place where money is occasionally kept has been left open.

She looks at Bobby's room. It is untouched. She feels sad. She remembers a photograph of herself and Bobby. In the photo, Bobby is a baby, lying tiny on an armchair. Ellen is a toddler standing next to the chair. She is pulling a face and baby Bobby is laughing. In the background their mother looks happily at her children. She looks young and beautiful.

Ellen imagines recreating the picture now. Bobby would be staring off to the side, with a blank expression. Ellen would be wearing modelling clothes and would not have even noticed her brother. Prudence would be looking morosely at her children, mascara running down her face, sobbing about some other misery. The picture would be printed onto a commemorative plate. Underneath the picture someone would have written 'A Modern Family: 2011'.

Ellen rings her mother to tell her about the robbery, but no-one answers the phone. She must be busy selling commemorative goods, thinks Ellen. She goes back down into the sitting room and sits next to her father on the sofa. She notices the pack of pills in front of him. She doesn't recognise the name of the painkiller.

She opens up the packaging and looks at her father. He is out for the count, she thinks. Inside the pack is a little pamphlet giving information about the pills. It says, do not take for more than three days in a row. Do not drive or operate heavy machinery whilst under the effects.

I can't drive and I don't need to operate heavy machinery, she thinks. May cause a dry mouth and fast heartbeat, the packaging says. Ellen goes to get a glass of water. She is not worried about having a fast heartbeat. I'm young, right, she thinks.

She takes one pill out of the blister pack. She thinks, my dad is less likely to notice if I take two pills out of the pack. She takes a second pill out. With a mouthful of water, she swallows the pills. Prudence is due back in a few hours.

Ellen looks at the money in her purse. She took out £70 from her modelling money today. She wanted to buy a simple dress for the fashion party but hadn't got round to it. £70 is nothing, she thinks. She looks at the queen's face on the twenty pound notes. The queen looks so proud of William and Kate. Slowly, a happy feeling of empathy settles over Ellen. She understands about the queen and about normal people.

She takes out a piece of paper and a pen and sits next to her father, her link to the first organism. She writes poem after poem.

hello queen
rule over us all
protect us

mum and dad
ellen and bobby
together

will and kate
commemorative
handsome plate

light like sound
comes to visit me
day and night

ceramic
just gonna love life
ceramic

Ellen looks at her father and feels fine. She doesn't need to
think about anything that she writes or worry about anything
she thinks. I can't wait for mum to get home, she thinks. And
my brother, she thinks. Love them both, she thinks.

* * *

How has your first week been?

Arnold Urnton is sitting on the work surface in the office
kitchen with his legs crossed and his hand daintily grasping
his right knee.

I think it's been very good, says Prudence. Ever since Arnold
mentioned that he'd have a chat to her this afternoon she has
been learning her figures. She knows that sales have increased
by 13% since last week.

Sales are up 13%, she says. I think that I am having a really
positive, motivational impact on the team.

You are doing a phenomenal job managing the team,
Prudence.

I really feel that we are all getting on with each other very well, says Prudence.

It's not long now, not long until the wedding. Do you think that you will be able to hit the targets we've set?

I think so. I mean, I'm putting my heart into it.

There's no pressure, Prudence. We know that it's a tough target and we know there is a lot to do. Just make sure that you do your best — that's all we ask.

Sure, says Prudence.

And then we'll see what happens after the wedding.

What happens after the wedding?

It depends what happens before the wedding.

Prudence is confused.

I don't understand, she says.

Oh don't worry about it Prudence, it's nothing to worry about. Your sales are up 13% for goodness sake — you really know how to get the most out of that motley crew!

Something about this feels dreadful, thinks Prudence.

Now go home and see your family. Relax. It's the weekend.

* * *

Inside this beautiful shopping centre, the shops stay open until eight o'clock in the evening. Bobby walks past HMV and WHSmith and Nando's and TopShop and TopMan and EAT and the Apple Store and Millie's Cookies and Waterstones and GAME and Office and Bella Italia and the food court featuring McDonalds Burger King KFC Pizza Hut Subway and Foot Locker and Boots and the Orange shop and Phones4U. He arrives at CEX.

He has a large bag with him. Inside are three DVD box sets, two old computer games and some CDs.

Bobby is pretty sure that he should be able to get the money he needs for a pre-paid game time card from the items. He also has a little money he found whilst frantically searching the house.

Whatever it costs me, it is worth it, he thinks.

Bobby thinks about what he would do to get the pre-paid game card. He thinks about whether he would cut his foot off. He thinks that he would. I don't care if I am in a wheelchair, he thinks. People in wheelchairs get looked after and they don't have to do jobs and people just give them free money and computers and World of Warcraft subscriptions, he thinks. I want to be a brain, plugged into a WoW server, he thinks. Maybe people would sponsor me, or come and watch me play, or make a documentary about me. Bobby thinks about a Channel 5 documentary called 'The Boy who is a Brain'.

It stars him, as a brain, sitting on a chair playing World of Warcraft.

What's the downside, he thinks.

CEX has very shiny red decorations, both outside and inside the shop. It has a queue of around twenty people waiting to either buy or sell consumer electronic equipment. The people look bored. Bobby joins the back of the queue. There are thousands of computer games, DVDs, CDs, consoles, laptops and phones in the shop. Some of the consumer electronics are turned on, and pump warm air into the room, making it hot. It smells like the inside of a computer in here.

At the counter, there is an argument going on. A customer is complaining about the value of the goods he is trying to trade in.

I just bought this last week, he says, it's new. It's definitely worth more than that – give me at least a fiver for it.

The lady behind the counter shakes her head slowly from side to side.

I'm going to take my business elsewhere then, says the man.

OK.

The customer seems irritated.

Bobby moves forward one space in the queue. Little beads of sweat are happening to his forehead. His phone keeps vibrating in his pocket. His family are trying to get hold of him. Leave me alone, thinks Bobby.

Finally at the counter, Bobby starts to unload the goods from his bag. The cashier looks at the goods, and waits as Bobby gets it all out.

Can I sell you this, he says.

The cashier looks at her wristwatch.

Bobby says again, can I sell you this.

The cashier remains silent for twenty seconds while looking at her wristwatch. Then she says, Oh sir I am sorry, it's just gone past the time when we can accept goods to buy back. You'll have to come back tomorrow.

Are you joking? says Bobby.

No, says the cashier, would you like to buy anything? We can still sell you items.

Bobby says, fuck you.

He picks up his items and throws them at the wall. A couple of the cases smash. He walks to a row of DVDs and pushes them all onto the floor. He throws five phones at the ceiling. What shall I do next, thinks Bobby.

* * *

Ellen and her father sit in chairs next to each other. They speak occasionally, giggling a little, discussing how certain beams of light strike certain objects in the room in a nice way.

Prudence looks at them and doesn't know what is happening. She hangs her jacket on the stick behind the door and turns and looks again at her husband and daughter.

Guys, she says.

They giggle.

Guys, she says.

Prudence goes and kneels down between the two of them. Ellen, she says. Husband, she says. Neither of them really move. Ellen nods a little. She looks a little like she is sleeping. The presenter also looks like he is sleeping.

Are you two OK, she says.

They remain silent.

Guys, she shouts at them.

Prudence feels lucky that Kate Middleton isn't here right now. If Kate were here right now it would be so embarrassing. She looks up at the commemorative plate. Kate's badly painted face glares down at her.

What happens after the royal wedding? thinks Prudence. Is this the Royal Wedding of my life, thinks Prudence. Will and Kate will take each other up the aisle. All of their friends and relations will be there, and then they will kiss each other, and the vibrations from her kiss will crash through the country and cross the waves and cause earthquakes and every time she sneezes or farts or just breathes a little slowly everyone in the world will discuss her as though they know her because they do know her because she belongs to everyone and everyone belongs to her.

Prudence walks over to the television presenter, and she slaps him in the face. He doesn't seem to notice. He is smiling. Then he says, I love you, Prudence.

Prudence doesn't know what to say to him. She looks at him for a while. Then her daughter says, I love you, mum.

Prudence doesn't know what to say to her.

Prudence sees the packet of painkillers on the table. She doesn't recognise the name of the painkillers. She wants to take one. She reads the information about the painkillers. She reads about the heavy machinery and the driving. She doesn't care.

Thirty minutes after taking the painkillers, Prudence is sitting comfortably in a chair. She is looking at the commemorative plate. She doesn't feel jealous. She looks at the brushwork on the plate. She thinks about each brush stroke and how it happened and why the artist did it. And she thinks about how unfair of her it was to criticise the workmanship on the plate. It's beautiful, she thinks. She wants to call her friend and tell her about the beautiful plate.

I want to paint commemorative plates about my own family, she thinks. I want to paint them in fantastic poses to show how wonderful each one of them is.

Where is Bobby, she thinks.

I love my son. He is a bully, because he is scared of no-one liking him. He doesn't work, because he wants to play. He buys pornography from a corner shop, because he has healthy, adolescent, sexual urges. He is perfect.

I know what I am, she thinks.

* * *

Twenty minutes later, Bobby arrives home from the shops. He rings the bell. No-one answers. He rings the bell again, then he realises that the door hasn't been properly locked. I want to destroy everything, he thinks. I want to rip doors off their hinges then I think that I want to masturbate about the female dwarf because I can't be with her in World of Warcraft.

Bobby pushes the door open. He is getting ready to apologise for searching frantically through all of the rooms of the house. He gets ready to think of some excuse as to why he needs money.

His family members sit together in the living room. They look stupefied. His mother is drooling and smiling. His father has his eyes closed, in an expression of confident bliss. His sister slowly moves her hand through her hair.

Um, thinks Bobby, desperately trying to think in terms of words and ideas, instead of just having an incomprehensible, unclassifiable reaction.

Um, he thinks again.

Bobby walks over to the family. He looks at each of them in turn. They say nothing. He says, hello.

Bobby's father opens his eyes.

I love you, son, he says.

Bobby's mother opens her eyes.

I love you, son, she says.

Bobby's sister opens her eyes.

I love you, brother, she says.

A small noise outside the house makes Bobby think of summer, and childhood. The painkillers are there on the table.

When am I going to have to apologise for my actions, he thinks. I want to play World of Warcraft, he thinks. My life is nothing, he thinks. I want to play World of Warcraft, he thinks. I want to be like my family, he thinks. My life is nothing, he thinks.

I just want someone to know what it's like to be me, he thinks.

He picks up the painkillers and looks at the packet. It says that the painkillers may cause drowsiness. I don't have to operate any heavy machinery soon, he thinks.

Bobby takes two painkillers with a glass of water. There are none left in the packet.

After taking the painkillers, Bobby spends half an hour collecting money from his parents' purses and wallets. He collects enough to buy a two-month World of Warcraft pre-paid game card. He feels really happy. Then he continues to feel really happy.

He moves back into the living room and moves a chair so that he is next to his family. He wants very badly to be near his family.

Tell me about the time before I existed, he says.

The television presenter looks at Bobby with tenderness, then looks at Prudence. They smile at each other. Yeah, I want to hear about it, too, says Ellen.

The family talk for hours before quietly falling asleep together. There are no pills left in the packet.

Part Four

Things happen around the presenter involving his agent and the ugly one and the small one. The things are sentences about being back at a place after not being there for a period of time. The presenter does his own things in reply and doesn't understand any of the things happening around him or because of him. He struggles.

Mandy has left the show. She said in her exit interview that she got a job somewhere else. Mandy has huge red waxy lips that will close around someone else's penis or mouth. Mandy is beeswax.

The world is coming to a slow halt. The sequence of events is stretching thinner and thinner, until nothing has any substance.

Major-league crab-crap.

Ultra-league bedbug-turds.

Meta-league human-shit.

There is a programme that needs to be made. It is a programme that is going to be cut together with the programme on the shittest roads in the world. They are going to splice them together so that the expensive footage of the Serbian roads is not completely wasted.

People keep telling the presenter not to worry.

They keep saying about how bad the accident was and that it's OK.

The presenter's brain works because others expect it to. His heart beats because others want it to beat.

I want painkillers, he thinks.

They plan things and make him make notes in a diary and talk about how soon he can go back to work. He feels like they want him to say that he is ready to go back to work as soon as possible, so he says it.

A new producer has started. She is younger than Mandy was. She wears tighter clothes and has cuter headphones that she always wears. She always wears her headphones and always talks into a small microphone stuck to her jaw.

The presenter thinks about the microphone in the same way that he thinks about lichen stuck to a rock, or barnacles to a ship.

The presenter's thoughts focus on getting more painkillers. It's not his fault, it's just what his brain is making him want. It's not his fault that he is incapable of doing anything that he is not compelled to do by his circumstances.

He calls his doctor's surgery and says that he needs to book an appointment to discuss medication. He's still with the others. They look at him as he speaks to the receptionist on the phone, seemingly having forgotten that he is with them.

The food on their table slowly reduces in quantity as they silently listen to the presenter talking to the receptionist. They feel embarrassed.

A song plays in the background. As the song plays, the presenter stops talking to the receptionist. He starts to listen to the songs carefully. And then, just as carefully, he starts to sing the words to the song. And then, tiny, beautiful tears form at his eyes and start to sparkle elegantly at his cheeks. He pushes his long grey hair backwards and cries.

The others looks embarrassed, and finish their meals.

* * *

Their legs seem to be swinging in unison. Did this happen by accident, thinks Ellen. Did I make mine swing in time with hers without realising? Will she notice and make a cruel joke about it?

Ellen makes a big effort to stop her legs swinging in time with Tracy's.

116

Are you going to watch the royal wedding? says Tracy.

My mum loves it, says Ellen. She is working on some kind of royal wedding promotion at the TV channel and it's sent her loopy. She won't stop going on about it. We've got loads of crap all over the house. You wouldn't believe some of it.

Tracy laughs.

Ellen loves her. All Ellen does is think about being able to tell Tracy what she is thinking.

They are both smoking. The wall they sit on is about five minutes away from school. They come here every morning break because smoking is banned at school. Smoking makes Ellen feel shit.

I have four days of shoots coming up, says Ellen, looking at the end of her cigarette, you won't see me until the party.

I bet the stylist is a prick, says Tracy.

I bet that he is secretly straight, says Ellen.

Tracy laughs.

He loves touching tits, says Tracy, he loves putting his head between women's tits and shaking it about and making a noise.

They laugh. Why is there no lipstick stuck to the end of my cigarette, thinks Ellen. She wonders whether lipstick on the end of a cigarette might be sexy.

It's sexy to me, thinks Ellen.

What shoots are you doing? says Tracy.

I don't know. The people at the agency just ring me and tell me where to go. I never really remember who it is that I am meant to be working with.

Ellen inhales for a long time on her cigarette. She coughs a few times. She looks at it and sees that she has smoked it all the way down to the filter. Her mouth tastes of dirty milk.

I want to lie down on a bed with you and talk to you about my life and tell you the secret things that I do and the secret things that I think about. I want to show you my private parts and I want to see your private parts. I want to kiss each other's private parts and feel comfortable around each other and love each other's private parts.

I want to take painkillers with you so that I can talk to you. I want to take painkillers and then I'll smoke with you and sit on the wall and do whatever you want because we'll be able to talk to each other then. When I don't have to filter my thoughts. When I don't have to think carefully about whether I should or shouldn't be thinking the things that I think. When I can just be, and we can just be together.

Ellen coughs again. Her mouth tastes of dirty milk.

My mouth tastes of dirty milk.

Let's go back in, it's time to learn, says Tracy.

What does Tracy want me to say, thinks Ellen.

Fuck time to learn, says Tracy.

* * *

Bobby is grinding Therazane rep for epic shoulder enchants.

He is chatting to the female dwarf while doing the Deepholm dailies. They chat about guild problems. There had been some drama between prominent guild members while Bobby was away. An in-game relationship got in the way of building a balanced raid team.

Bobby slowly starts to think, we are talking about in-game relationships.

He types, they can be just as real as irl relationships, I guess.

I guess, says the female dwarf.

They haven't talked that much to each other about their private lives.

Do you play any other games? she asks.

I used to, but I only really play WoW now, says Bobby.

What do you do, apart from WoW?

I work with computers but its really boring, says Bobby. Why can't I just tell her the truth, he thinks. He thinks about Harriet in school. He had really liked Harriet. She was quiet and kind.

Bobby feels like he was dishonest with Harriet because he had acted like a jerk with her.

Do you think that whatever you do, that's what you are, says Bobby.

What do you mean? says the female dwarf.

I mean, like, because I just work with computers, does that mean that all I am is a guy who works with computers, even if it doesn't feel that way to me in my heart, says Bobby.

No. I think that you are whatever you feel like. What sort of ambitions do you have?

I don't know, that's the problem, I guess. That's why I'm just nothing, because I don't feel like anything.

Ha, says the female dwarf.

I hate Deepholm dailies. They are so fucking boring, says Bobby.

They are not as bad as the firelands dailies oh my god! says the female dwarf.

I'm not up to those yet, says Bobby. It's dark in Deepholm, and he can see his reflection in the computer screen. He doesn't feel like anything.

Would you come to a guild meet-up if one was ever organised? says the female dwarf.

Haha I don't know, says Bobby.

I would go I think. It would be nice to meet you and some of the others.

I don't know I feel weird about it, says Bobby.

OK, says the female dwarf.

Bobby types, I really like you, then deletes the words from the dialogue bar.

* * *

On the wall in Prudence's office are many royal wedding posters. There are red, white and blue paper chains looping from the corners of the room to the centre and dangling down a little. Will and Kate stand in a hundred different, similar ways, smiling, cradling each other. A pile of papers lie on Prudence's desk. They are unprocessed sales dockets. In order for them to count toward the figures of the sales team, they need to be processed, input onto the system, put into a special drawer. She needs to be on a particular part of the company intranet in order to start processing the orders.

Her web browser is at www.willandkate.blogspot.com.

She looks at articles about getting a first glimpse at Kate's wedding dress. She feels angry. She looks at pictures of Will's odd, pumpkin face and contorted, toothy smile.

When I was young, he might have been interested in me, she thinks. She remembers what she looked like in her wedding dress, with the presenter at her side. All she had thought throughout the wedding had been, is this it. The royal wedding moment of her life hasn't happened yet.

She navigates to www.heatmagazine.co.uk. Every story on the website is about the royal wedding. There are articles about the most fashionable wedding physique. There are articles about male grooming, with regards to it now being acceptable to be male and to groom. There are articles about the mother-of-the-bride not upstaging the bride by trying to look too young. There are articles about working to co-ordinate the outfits that your wedding guests wear. There are articles about what to do if a wedding guest has too much to drink. There are articles about choosing the perfect first dance song that is equally romantic, ironic, heartfelt, meaningful and musically interesting.

The article says that the ultimate song to play as the first dance at a wedding is *Always* by Erasure.

Prudence goes to YouTube and plays *Always* by Erasure. She goes to another website that allows you to loop YouTube videos. She listens to the song on loop.

She looks again at the images of the possibly-leaked wedding dress and pictures of Will's pumpkin face. She takes a block of staples out of a small box on her desk. She presses one of the ends of the block of staples into her arm until she can feel the pain start. She reads more and more articles about the wedding, whilst pressing the sharp block into her arm. She doesn't feel good. She doesn't feel like she is controlling anything or that her life is more manageable. She just feels pain. She pushes a little harder and rubs the block back and forth a little. Blood starts to come out of her arm.

There is a knock at her door.

Whatever, she thinks.

Mr. Urnton comes in. She hides her arm, but it looks odd. It looks a lot like she is trying to hide her arm from him, for some reason.

She pauses *Always* by Erasure.

Everything OK, Prudence, he says.

Just fine, she replies, trying to smile.

Sales for the day are looking a little thin, so I thought I'd come and check whether there had been any problems.

Oh no, it's fine, I have some dockets to process, it's been a little hectic.

I see. Make sure to stay on top of the paperwork Prudence, we can't have the team's hard work going to waste!

Of course, she says.

Prudence knows that blood from her cut has almost certainly smeared itself on her skirt, or at least on her shirt sleeve. As Mr. Urnton turns to leave, Prudence thinks, when am I going to grow out of this behaviour. As the door closes behind him, she realises that she will never grow out of anything.

She unpauses *Always* by Erasure, and picks up the staples again.

* * *

The receptionist at the surgery tells the presenter that his normal doctor is not available today.

Um, says the presenter.

But don't worry, Dr. Younis is fantastic.

Um, says the presenter.

Instead of sitting down, he remains standing in front of the receptionist's desk. There is a fly in the room, zooming around his head and occasionally landing on his nose.

Would you like to sit down? says the receptionist.

I don't mind, says the presenter. The other waiters in the room look at him, a little uncomfortably. He doesn't realise that anyone in the room is uncomfortable. He stands for a few more seconds and then goes to sit in a chair that faces the window. As he looks through the window he thinks that the world looks very far away.

Shortly, he is moved into the doctor's room, where Dr. Younis does a professional examination of the presenter's leg.

It still hurts? says the doctor.

Yes, says the presenter.

It's amazing, it really looks fine to me. The break should definitely have healed by now. Where exactly does it hurt?

The leg, says the presenter.

The whole leg? says the doctor.

Both legs and my groin and feet, says the presenter.

Right, says the doctor, there must be some bruising I suppose. It's nothing that I am worried about in terms of you having a chronic condition or anything. I will just prescribe some more pain management medication and we'll see how you are in a week. I'd like you to take less though, only when it is completely unbearable. This medicine is not good for you.

I know, I hate taking it, says the presenter.

So don't take it all the time or you'll run out early.

I'll try not to take any, says the presenter.

They talk a little more, and the doctor appears to make notes on a website that looks like Wikipedia, and then he prints a prescription off and signs it.

The presenter is thinking about the quickest possible way to drive to the pharmacy.

I think that for convenience, you should have a pharmacy built into the surgery, says the presenter.

It's useful for older people, I suppose, says the doctor. By the way, when does the new series of your car show start.

The television presenter wants to say, hopefully never. He wants to say, I want to die whenever I think about doing that work. He wants to say, can I have a job handing out pamphlets to people giving information about yearly flu jabs. He wants to say, let me clean your toilet and live here and never look at another car, or a lad.

He says, I don't know, a month or something.

I just love the banter on the show, says the doctor. You guys are all just such great lads.

One hour later the presenter sits in a chair, thinking wonderful thoughts about every element of his existence.

* * *

Ellen puts on lipstick. She looks at a picture of fashion models on the internet. She finds pictures of herself being a fashion model on the internet.

She sits down and cries about her life then stands up and walks downstairs. She walks back upstairs. She looks at her text messages. She texts the lead singer and tells him to come to the party. She texts the man she keeps having sex with and tells him to come to the party. She reads all of her old text messages.

There are a lot of messages from Tracy. When she reads a message from Tracy she feels great. Her text messages are her diary. They are a way for her to know what other people think of her. She hasn't saved her outgoing messages.

She goes downstairs. Her dad is on painkillers, doing a drawing from a photograph of Bobby. The drawing is very good. My dad loves Bobby, thinks Ellen.

Ellen goes and knocks on Bobby's door.

Bobby doesn't answer.

She tries to open the door. It's locked. Can't be bothered, she thinks. She thinks about the photograph of the modern family. She feels like she could cry again. She laughs a little, her thoughts mashing together in an incomprehensible mix.

She decides that she must tell Tracy how she feels about her. It's not fair to anyone for her only feeling in life to be a pathetic, unfulfilled love. Ellen wants to burn everything down and sit in the ashes and do nothing.

Downstairs, her father plays *The Chain* by Fleetwood Mac. He sings along to the words and hums along to the music.

She wants to write a poem, but can't. She writes down:

let me see those bangers.
let me see those bangers.
let me see those bangers.

A text message arrives. It is a surprise. It is from the lead singer. The text message says: I know you've been cheating on me with lots of people. Why do you treat me like this? I love you.

Ellen thinks about the text message and isn't interested in it. Her only thought is of Tracy. All she cares about is being with her all of the time.

She calls Tracy. She is ready to tell her about the way she feels. She imagines Tracy lying next to her and telling her that she is a wonderful lover. She imagines the two of them in love.

She says, Tracy the lead singer has texted me, what should I do?

* * *

Mandy is unemployed. She sits at home and applies for new jobs. She pays her rent from her savings. She has nightmares about the presenter's penis. She tells her friends that she had sex with an A-list celeb and that it was amazing and that the celeb was dynamite in the sack. She goes on websites to connect with her friends. She tags herself in photographs. She goes to job centres. She prints out little bits of paper in the job centres. She speaks to her parents on the phone. She thinks about living at home. She thinks about starting a family. She shops at a variety of supermarkets and sometimes buys clothes. She drinks wine in the evenings. She is the most miserable human being alive in the world. She is the happiest, most fulfilled person alive. She sits on the floor in her room, looking at her sofa, thinking, what's the point. She lies face down on the carpet and falls asleep.

* * *

Bobby masturbates in the bath. He doesn't enjoy ejaculating. He eats dinner and doesn't enjoy eating. He imagines letting the food drop out of his mouth and then smiling at his mother and father and sister and then dropping onto the floor and doing forward rolls.

He is waiting to go and play on the computer.

He plays on the computer.

The next day is school. He goes to the classes and thinks about playing on the computer. His friends tell him about television and music. He avoids talking as much as possible and goes to the toilet a few times and at break-time he walks a very specific route around the least populated areas of the school. He learnt the route from a boy with autism who sometimes sits in the library typing novels out backwards. He followed the boy around on his route, staying 100m behind him.

I want autism and do I already have it, thought Bobby.

Then he is at home.

He eats dinner and doesn't talk about his day when his family ask him.

He plays on the computer.

He has reached 18,796 rep with Therazane. FFS he thinks. His ilvl is 345. He wants his ilvl to be higher so that he can enter higher level dungeons.

The female dwarf raids often. Bobby wants to be with her online as much as possible.

She compliments him. She calls him funny. She does emoticons at him. She does links to YouTube at him. She does links to jpgs and gifs to him. They interact.

Bobby falls asleep at his desk.

Then he eats breakfast.

Then he goes to school.

There are some exams coming up in a few months. Everyone is talking about them. A teacher calls Bobby into a room and tells him that he is a bad boy and needs to do more work. Bobby thinks about the computer.

He thinks about the female dwarf living in the computer. She doesn't really live in the computer, he thinks.

GCSE says the teacher.

Bobby goes home and has dinner and doesn't enjoy it. He masturbates in the bathroom and doesn't enjoy it. He sits at the computer and talks to the female dwarf. They talk about life. They talk about the graphics of World of Warcraft. They both think that the graphics are good. They both think that stylised graphics are great because they are accessible. But they can still be epic. They both type the word epic a lot.

They reroll new chars together. They both pick gnomes. They quest together for three hours. The female dwarf says that they should get a Ventrilo server. Bobby says that he doesn't have a mic. The female dwarf says that she will buy a mic for him and send it to him. Bobby wants to kiss the female dwarf's avatar on screen.

It's weird, you being a gnome, Bobby says.

Ha, says the female dwarf.

I'm used to your other char, he says.

Yeah, says the female dwarf.

Is this useful for you, says Bobby. He trades a BOE item with her.

Um, I want to tell you something, says the female dwarf.

Ok, says Bobby.

I am in love with you, I think, says the female dwarf.

Um, thinks Bobby.

Sorry, says the female dwarf.

Um, thinks Bobby.

Don't worry, says the female dwarf.

She logs off.

Bobby stares at the screen for hours, grinding more rep.

* * *

Parcels keep arriving for Prudence. She keeps all of the packaging that they arrive in in a special room. She likes reading her name on the packages. They are just for her. The packages come from her TV channel.

Prudence is preparing a special surprise for her family. She puts things up on the walls and arranges ornaments in particular ways. She hates what she is doing. She wants to coat herself in razors and shred the contents of the room she is preparing. She carefully picks up a beautiful porcelain figure of Will and puts it on a handsome plinth. She picks up the corresponding Kate porcelain figure and stands it next to her prince.

She sits at her computer. She goes onto recipe websites and does research into royal weddings from the past. Coronation chicken, she thinks. She tries to find a good recipe for coronation chicken. People weren't used to spices in the old days, apparently, so the old fashioned recipes can be a little bland for today's sophisticated palates.

She finds an article which tries to scientifically find the perfect recipe for coronation chicken. It lists a few different recipes and describes what's good and bad about them. She picks the one that the article tells her is best.

She takes a sheet of Will and Kate special paper and writes out, in lovely handwriting, the recipe for coronation chicken. I am going to practise it, she thinks. She stabs the pen into her arm and starts bleeding. She smiles at the recipe and the idea of practising the coronation chicken recipe.

I need to practise it one hundred times before the wedding, she thinks. That's impossible, she thinks, laughing and hurting herself a lot with the pen. The royal wedding is the royal wedding of my life, she thinks. Everyone else's life is the royal wedding of my life, she thinks. Putting things in my arm is the royal wedding of my life, she thinks.

She types into Google, MAIL ORDER CHICKEN LARGE QUANTITY.

After looking through a few pages, she finds a company that can satisfy her requirements. She orders fifty chickens. She types into Google LARGE CHICKEN FREEZER.

* * *

On the interview set of his television programme, as the presenter speaks to a famous woman, he decides to maim himself in order to secure a reliable source of painkillers. He decides to do it mid-question. He stops talking and the famous woman looks at him. He has stopped thinking about anything except the feelings that he is able to experience whilst the painkillers affect him.

Um, says the presenter.

He thinks about how he is going to do it, and he is deliriously happy.

They are filming a special show about destroying caravans in a week. He is going to get his arm caught in a hydraulic press and have it completely maimed. Little angels sing inside his head. They have flutes. He says, um, and looks oddly fish-like, his wavy grey locks curtains around his enraptured face.

Are you OK? says the famous woman.

I'm in a great mood, thank you, says the television presenter.

What's going on? she whispers.

The television presenter smiles and shrugs his shoulders. He smiles very widely and opens his mouth as he smiles.

The famous woman smiles a very broad, terrified smile. The crowd around them laugh a little and then slowly fall silent.

Someone coughs. The presenter and the famous woman stare at each other for a minute, and then he says, what was the question.

The new producer of the show walks onto the stage and bustles around, making everything alright. The audience are sent home. The famous woman goes and sits in the green room and drinks brandy. The presenter is interrogated by the production team. They ask him questions about his mental state. The presenter tries to answer their questions so that they don't kick him off the show. It's important to him that he stays on the show so that he can maim his arm in a hydraulic press and get a lifetime's supply of painkillers.

I'm fine, he says.

It's funny, he says.

She's weird or something, he says.

The production team make notes together and humour the presenter. He tells them how excited he is to be working on new shows with the team.

They decide that he is OK, for the time being.

The famous woman stumbles out of the green room, vomits on the ground, starts crying like a baby, drinks more brandy, falls asleep.

* * *

The neon signs tell the people in the bar that it is a cool place that is exclusive and interesting. The lead singer chose it as the place to meet. He said that it was their place. Ellen barely remembers being here with him before. She is waiting to go outside and have a cigarette. The lead singer is crying.

You make me hate myself, he says.

Um, says Ellen.

You make me feel like a bad person. You make me feel guilty for wanting to be with you. You make me feel like a liar even though I have never lied to you.

Hunks of snot and cups of tears cover his face. His haircut, normally full of volume and vigour, lies flat across his head. He is wearing unfashionable clothes.

I didn't really know that we were going out, or that you had any feelings for me at all, says Ellen

The lead singer lets out a gut-wrenching howl and collapses face down on the table. He beats the surface, sending glasses smashing out in all directions.

We only really saw each other a few times, Ellen says.

The lead singer brings his face up and looks into Ellen's eyes.

I'm coming to the celebrity stylist party. We can have a nice time together. The rest of the band are going to be there as well. We always have a good time when we are together, don't we?

Whatever you like, says Ellen, I am going to have a cigarette outside.

The lead singer follows her outside. He compliments her on her looks and the way she holds a cigarette.

I hold it just in a normal way, says Ellen.

Yeah, that's what I like, he laughs.

Ellen thinks, I would act like this around Tracy if it would make her love me. All I care about is other people, she thinks.

Ellen tries briefly to understand what the lead singer is, and what he means. She looks at him. She wants to feel something about him, but can't.

She smokes her cigarette in silence. The singer crouches a little, as if expecting her to speak at any moment. He occasionally flinches, as though hearing something and preparing to react. As he realises each time that Ellen has said nothing, he returns to his odd crouch, blinking and looking at the ground.

Ellen thinks about how difficult life is for everyone and then thinks that there is no such thing as difficult.

* * *

The female dwarf has not been online for a few days. Bobby has got into the habit of logging on briefly, checking his friends list, logging off, logging back in twenty minutes later. He wishes he could get an application for his phone that would let him know whenever she came on.

He checks round the clock. He is worried about her.

And then, one evening, late, at about eleven-thirty, her name pops up in his list of friends.

He whispers to her, hello.

She doesn't reply.

She is in Stormwind.

He is in Darnassus.

He activates his hearthstone and teleports to Stormwind.

He whispers to her again, hello.

She doesn't reply.

He is sweating and feels out of control.

He types /y HELLO.

His words sound in the public chat channel of Stormwind. Tens of people write to him telling him to shut up and fuck off. Others yell back at him HELLO. The female dwarf says nothing.

He yells again, I FEEL THE SAME WAY.

People in the SW chat channel laugh at him. They tell him to fuck off again. The female dwarf says nothing. He whispers to her one more time. He says, I'm sorry I didn't say anything the other day. I felt scared. I feel the same way, but I just feel scared about it.

Don't be scared, says the female dwarf.

I can't help it, I think, says Bobby.

He is running around Stormwind, trying to find the female dwarf. She is not near the main auction house. She is not near the auction house in the Dwarven district.

Where are you, Bobby says.

The female dwarf invites him into a group with her. Her position appears on Bobby's map. She is by the daily fishing quest-giver. He mounts his drake and flies over to her. She is fishing. He stands next to her and takes his fishing rod out.

He casts the rod into the canal and listens for the splash that indicates the hooking of a fish.

He hears the splash. The female dwarf has also hooked a fish. They reel in together. They fish in silence for a few minutes.

I really want to meet you, says the female dwarf.

I don't think I can, says Bobby.

I don't want to regret not even seeing if it would work between us.

I can't, says Bobby.

The two fish in silence for two more minutes.

Please, says the female dwarf.

Bobby puts off answering. He stands up and turns away from the computer. He puts his hands on his hips and breathes out. He thinks that he feels like an adult with his hands on his hips.

He sits back down. I am really ugly, he types.

Why are you saying that? I want to see you.

Ok – you said that it doesn't matter what you are, it's what you feel like that is important, right?

Of course.

You believe that?

Yes, Bobby.

I'm 15 years old but I am in love with you.

WHAT THE FUCK?

* * *

Hi I'm ill can't come into work today because of food poisoning, says Prudence.

Prudence is everything OK? says Arnold Urnton.

No, I have food poisoning, says Prudence, I'm very ill and won't be in for a few days I think.

Her voice is bright and clear.

Hmm, says Arnold. Please phone me at the end of the day and let me know...

Prudence puts the phone down. I don't need no fucking job, she thinks, laughing internally. She laughs a little externally. Her eyes look extremely happy.

She walks into the kitchen. There is red, white and blue bunting hanging from the ceiling in generous loops. There are images of Will and Kate on the wall. Her huge freezer has arrived. It's full of her chicken. She opens the fridge. Inside is a chicken from last night, defrosted. She touches the inner parts of the chicken to make sure it's warmed all the way through. The flesh feels like Arnold Urnton's hand. She puts the chicken on a kitchen surface. Next to the chicken is a pile of different recipes for coronation chicken. She thinks to herself, one a day, until the big day.

She puts a big pan of water on to boil. While the water heats, she hacks at the chicken with a knife. Small pieces of skin, flesh and bone shoot across the room, imperceptible to Prudence. She whistles the national anthem as she hacks.

After the water boils, she puts the pieces of chicken into the pan, and cuts into her arm a little with the knife from the chicken. She hums the song *Always*, by Erasure. As she cuts, she thinks that she barely knows who the television presenter is. She tries to remember the four-hour period that they shared together after they had taken painkillers, but she can't.

She thinks nothing as she toasts hot curry powder in a good quality non-stick pan. She uses a wooden spoon to keep the Teflon coating intact. Blood from her arm lands in cute spots on the floor.

In a bowl she whisks drops of olive oil into egg yolk until a delicious mayonnaise forms. She adds the toasted curry powder and throws in some plump raisins. After the chicken is cooked she tears the hot flesh into strips and coats them with the mayonnaise.

She wants to cry but can't. She wishes that Wills and Kate could see the fantastic efforts she is going to. She hates Wills and Kate and wants to be more important and loved than the two of them.

She adds a little parsley to the mix and flamboyantly flings a few drops of Worcester sauce on top.

Who can I ring about this, she thinks. She thinks about her husband, her children, her friends. She is too weak and pathetic to use the phone. She sits in front of the television and eats the coronation chicken. She watches a programme about the royal wedding.

None of her family members have said a word to her about the royal wedding. They don't give a shit about the heritage and values of our fantastic country and our wonderful royal family, she thinks. I am going to make them care, she thinks. I am going to make them care a lot about the royal wedding and make them respect our royal family and make them respect the history and values of this country.

* * *

This caravan is an abomination, reads the presenter from an autocue. He points at a caravan and flicks his long hair out of his face. It is a very bad caravan, he ad-libs. The audience of one thousand billion at home laugh themselves to insanity.

Stick to the autocue, says the new producer.

Um, says the presenter.

Start again, says the new producer.

This caravan is an abomination, says the presenter. It is a rusting bucket of bad bolts and rubbish shit, says the presenter.

Very good, mouths the producer.

We are going to crush the caravan in a hydraulic press because we hate it, says the presenter. He is sweating a little because of the bright studio lights. He doesn't care what he looks like. Want to take a painkiller and be able to express myself, he thinks.

The hydraulic press is extremely massive. It is big enough to crush a large, American-style, Winnebago-type caravan.

How am I going to get my arm into it, thinks the presenter.

Time to crush the caravan, says the producer. She compliments the presenter on his introduction.

Should I pretend to get caught in the hydraulic press, says the presenter.

No, that sounds dangerous, says the producer. Stay away from it.

The small one and the ugly one are watching the hydraulic press, laughing about something between themselves. The television presenter doesn't feel angry or annoyed or hurt by their laughter. It just doesn't register with him. Nothing registers with him except the thought 'put your hand in the press' and 'get some painkillers to make life bearable'.

As the press fires up, the presenter takes small steps towards it. It's making a loud noise as the caravan starts to be compressed. There are two cameras filming the buckling metal. It looks like a rose, curling into itself. It is covered in oil and lovely fluids. The caravan eats itself. It is like a vagina, eating itself, thinks the presenter. I want to put my hand in that vagina as it eats itself, thinks the presenter.

He is almost close enough. The producer is shouting something at him but it's too late. He can feel little splashes of oil and metal touching his hand.

He says, OH GOD I THINK I AM IN THE MIDDLE OF AN INDUSTRIAL ACCIDENT, and then he falls toward the press, on purpose, and his left hand is caught in the self-destroying metal vagina of the caravan.

Immediately, he is in pain. It's not really like any pain he has ever felt before. Oh well, he thinks. The pain becomes worse. His hand is not being crushed exactly, but impaled, scratched, put under pressure, ripped a little, shredded. Bits of car are doing very bad things to his hand.

OH GOD HOW DID THIS HAPPEN, he says, calmly.

People around him start to panic. The producer talks manically into her mouthpiece, bouncing from side to side like an odd child's toy. The ugly one and the small one appear from nowhere. They chatter, repulsed, and point a little at the injured arm. They seem really worried about it.

The presenter, grinning, remembers to seem concerned. He tries very hard to frown, but has forgotten how to do it properly. Half of his face slumps, the other half remains the same, giving him a simpering, cheeky appearance. He fights for control of his eyebrows. He thinks about doing a thumbs-up with his other hand. I have never been in this situation before, he thinks. I wonder what Mandy is doing at the moment, he thinks.

An ambulance arrives and people make a fuss of him. Some blood is everywhere. People lie him down and put him in the ambulance and attach him to things that put things into his bloodstream.

Jackpot, he thinks.

He stares up at the ceiling of the ambulance. He perceives things. He is carrying out his function. I am nothing, he thinks, with happy sincerity and joyous liberation.

* * *

Children shout swear words at Bobby as he walks up a hill at school. He smells bad. He looks bad. He feels like he doesn't want to be there.

A teacher sees him walking up the hill and walks toward him. Bobby Martin, she says.

Yes, says Bobby.

Are you alright? says the teacher.

Yes, says Bobby.

Come with me, Bobby, let's have a quick chat.

I'm going to be late, says Bobby.

It doesn't matter, come with me.

They walk together towards the teacher's office. She notices that Bobby smells very bad. He smells stale and slightly sweet in a rancid, curdled way. Bobby doesn't make eye contact with anyone he passes. He keeps his head down. He accidentally bumps into another student. His bag falls off and pornographic magazines fall out.

The teacher helps Bobby to put the magazines back into his bag. I need to feel worried, thinks the teacher.

When they reach the teacher's office, Bobby Martin stands up in front of her desk as she sits down.

Am I in trouble, says Bobby.

No Bobby, she says, I just want to talk about things with you. Why don't you sit down?

He clumsily puts his bag down on the ground and slowly lowers himself into the chair in the room. His body is slumped uncomfortably forward. His shoulders are rounded and he looks down at the ground. The teacher thinks that it is her professional duty to feel concerned about Bobby Martin.

Bobby, is everything OK at home? How is your father?

Fine, I think he got his hand caught in a mangle or something.

Oh dear. Is it hard for your mother to look after you at the moment?

No, says Bobby.

Bobby, I'm going to tell you a few things. They are not criticisms, they are just observations. You tell me if you think that they are fair.

Bobby doesn't say anything. His eyes remain fixed on a point on the floor.

It looks like you are not really taking care of yourself at the moment Bobby. Is that fair?

Don't know, says Bobby. He thinks to himself, what is taking care of yourself.

You smell bad Bobby. It's important for people your age to keep a healthy habit of showering every day. It's part of growing up.

Right, says Bobby. I'm not growing up, he thinks.

You need to start looking after yourself a little more because it sounds like your parents are having trouble at the moment.

It's tough on your mother with your father being injured, she needs all of your help.

Why can't I decide on a trade like being a blacksmith or professionally skinning animals and tanning their hides and just do that and not be bothered by the teacher and live in a hut in the woods and have a female dwarf that lives with me, thinks Bobby. I don't want parents and I don't want school and I don't want anything that this world can offer me.

I want all parts of my life to be represented by small, slowly filling bars that give me objective, tangible rewards when they finally fill, thinks Bobby.

Right, says Bobby.

* * *

Stop talking to me, thinks Ellen.

Everyone is beautiful, says the celebrity stylist.

Um, says Ellen.

She misses not being around the stylist. She thinks back with intense fondness about the time that she wasn't with him. A celebrity comes and talks to them briefly, spilling a little of their drink on the floor. The stylist puts his hand on the celebrity's hip. Ellen doesn't care about anything that is happening.

I need to find Tracy, she thinks.

I'm going, she says.

Don't go, says the stylist, you are fabulous.

No, I have to go.

Ellen calls Tracy. She is in another part of the party. It sounds loud. She finds her and they drink five shots of a drink. The lead singer is there. He is crying about not being Ellen's boyfriend. Ellen is drunk and she tells him that they never even went out, fuck off, I took a morning-after pill for you you piece of shit, it's bad for my hormones.

Tracy laughs.

Ellen laughs.

Ellen feels very close to Tracy.

They have five more shots of a drink.

The lead singer has gone somewhere else. The man who got the tickets for Ellen is nearby. He keeps looking at Ellen. He wants to have sex with her again because she is beautiful. She tells Tracy that his sexual technique is inadequate. Ellen laughs. She has slender arms and soft eyes, thinks Tracy.

I am going to get a tattoo of your name on my arm, says Ellen. Tracy blinks her eyes. The blink seems to last a long time. Her eyelashes stick together a little. A wave of movement makes the flesh of her lids spring apart with a soft tension. It takes a moment for her eyes to take their normal size again. They are a shape and colour that makes Ellen feel like wreathing herself in cigarette smoke and exploding. I want to get a tattoo of your eyes on my eyelids, says Ellen.

Tracy laughs.

I want to get a tattoo of your arms up my arms and across my shoulder blades, says Ellen.

I want to get a tattoo of your lips on my lips, Ellen says.

I want a tattoo of your name on my arm, says Tracy.

Ellen moves a little closer to Tracy and puts her hand on her hip. Her job is to experience lust that some parts of the universe feel for other parts of the universe that some other parts of the universe feel is inappropriate. Her job is to catalogue and process this lust, fleetingly, through experience. Her job is to pass this processed lust on to others directly, through self-expression, and indirectly, through action and lifestyle.

Tracy. I feel things for you. Do you know that, says Ellen.

Yes, of course I know.

No, I really feel things for you.

Ellen applies a little more pressure to Tracy's hip. It is a noticeably unusual amount of pressure.

I feel really very strongly about you and I think that my feelings are more than friend feelings but I get it if you don't feel the same way because it's weird so it's OK and we can still be best friends if you view me as a best friend because I definitely view you as my best friend I just really wanted to tell you because this one time we nearly kissed and for me at least it was the best thing that ever happened like it was an accident we kissed cheeks but I sort of accidentally brushed your lips with mine and it felt so incredible I wanted to kiss you and we could at least see if it feels weird or whatever I just don't care about modelling or celebrity stylists or drugs or famous people or anything at all except you, Ellen says.

Tracy puts her hand on Ellen's hand. She holds Ellen's fingers. She moves her face close to Ellen's face.

I love you, says Tracy. She kisses Ellen's mouth. They hold each other. Her hand is on her lower back. Her lips stab her skin and squirt ink under the surface, tattooing themselves onto the flesh wherever they land. Lines move over their bodies. They breathe strongly and irregularly. Their mouths taste of nothing to each other.

* * *

Prudence picks the presenter up from the hospital. He has a large supply of painkillers and is in a wheelchair. He seems very happy in his wheelchair.

I don't need this wheelchair, he says, but it's fun!

The doctor said something about it to us, says Prudence. She is annoyed that this is taking time out from her coronation chicken practice sessions. She thinks about the right thing to ask a husband whose hand has been mangled.

Um, she says.

How did it happen, she says.

Accidental mangling, says the presenter, I didn't realise that the crusher was there.

Oh dear, says Prudence. She is thinking about adding toasted almonds to the coronation chicken. Got to make sure that they are toasted properly. They will add a lovely sweet note. Remember to reduce the amount of raisins accordingly, Prudence. I am going to tailor this meal to the modern palate extremely elegantly, she thinks. She imagines cutting a knife across her thighs.

I'm going to make a big deal out of the royal wedding – I want us all to watch it together and cheer on Wills and Kate, says Prudence.

OK, says the presenter. The presenter thinks about the idea of having a wife. What do you do after you know everything about each other, he thinks. Never mind, he thinks.

Who is getting married? he says.

Wills and Kate, says Prudence. The best young couple and the monarchy's best hope for the future, she says.

She pushes the presenter into the car park. It always rains in the hospital car park.

The car looks very beautiful, says the presenter. It has a very cute, elegant, stylish finish. It looks like a continuation of the ground, flowing from its start-point to its destination. I am seeing it in four dimensions.

I have been practising my coronation chicken. It's the traditional dish of the royal wedding. They served it at the last royal wedding, says Prudence. I have lots of items from work, says Prudence. I quit the job, says Prudence.

What are our children doing these days?

Getting ready for the royal wedding, says Prudence.

I love our family. It's our connection to eternity, says the presenter.

That is very sentimental and weird, says Prudence.

She opens the car door.

In you get, she says.

I want to kiss you and passionately make love with you like the day I was hungover, says the presenter.

Prudence doesn't know what to say. She pretends not to hear the presenter. She looks around and thinks about what people do when they haven't heard something. She whistles a little. She taps her thigh with her hand. She taps her foot. I want to have a panic attack, she thinks.

The presenter forgets what he was thinking about and starts singing a song about the old days in England. He exists in a wonderful context-less moment.

On the way home he opens the window and puts his head outside, letting rain wash his forehead, hair and eyes.

* * *

The next morning, they will lie next to each other, on white sheets in a cheap hotel room. They will both pretend to be asleep for a long time, not wanting to speak to the other. Ellen will feel absolutely nothing. She will not want to look at Tracy. She will not feel fulfilled. She will not feel happy. She won't feel sad. She will just want to leave. Then she will leave. Tracy will lie on the bed, thinking that she should be crying, being unable to cry.

On her way home, Ellen will think to herself, what shall I choose to become fixated with now.

* * *

Bobby sits on his chair, looking on the internet for other computer games that he can play. He is on steam. He thinks about downloading the demos of a few different games, but doesn't bother. The free demos all seem very bad.

He stands up, walks to the wall and stands by it for ten minutes. He can hear the sound of the world outside his window. The world sounds like rain falling onto cement.

He thinks about the female dwarf. He walks across the room to another wall and stands by it for five minutes. He wonders what it is like to be the female dwarf. He thinks about what it is like to be someone other than himself or the female dwarf. Should I scream, he thinks. Should I lie on the floor, he thinks.

I want to scream and lie on the floor together with the female dwarf, he thinks.

He walks out of his room and down the stairs. There is his mother, cooking coronation chicken. There is his sister, sitting next to her phone, drinking gin. There is his father, cradling his mangled hand, talking to himself.

Bobby says, I am having romance problems.

His family don't move. They remain engrossed in themselves.

Could anyone talk to me about my romance problems, says Bobby, not particularly waiting for an answer.

I have fallen in love with an older woman on World of Warcraft, which I am not allowed to play. I initially told her that I was older than I really am. She fell in love with me, I think. Eventually I told her that I am fifteen and she went berserk. She sent me really hurtful in-game mail and hasn't logged on since. She told everyone in the guild that I am a liar and I got kicked out. What should I do, says Bobby.

You are in trouble, says the television presenter. Then he says, just kidding, um.

Prudence wafts a plate of coronation chicken in front of Bobby's nose. She says, the royal wedding is tomorrow – eat this chicken to practise. Bobby notices that the living room is entirely coated in bunting and images of Will and Kate. Some of the pictures have been drawn by Prudence.

His sister starts crying then laughs briefly then remains still for a moment and then says, I want to do something else. She holds her hands out in front of her briefly, claws the air, then collapses on the table.

Bobby tries to think about whether he is more upset about not being able to play World of Warcraft, or not being able to interact with the female dwarf then he thinks neither is important.

In front of the television presenter are many blister packs full of painkillers.

* * *

It is early on the day of the royal wedding of William and Kate, the most incredible day in the history of Great Britain. Birds fly in swooping symphonies across the sky and below them, the subjects of the United Kingdom of Great Britain, Scotland, Northern Ireland and Wales are uniformly joyous as they celebrate their benevolent betters, the royal family.

In a proudly kept household in the north of the kingdom, a family sits around the breakfast table. They each have in front of them a plate of scrambled eggs and bacon. They drink warm coffee and cold orange juice. They talk tenderly to each other about their feelings and failings, their experiences, their understanding of life. The family all started the day off by taking the correct dosage of extremely strong prescription painkiller.

The father says, I hate being defined by my work.

The mother says, although I understand why that would be a concern, I urge you not to worry about it.

The son says, you are my father and your work is unimportant to me.

The daughter says, I have never really thought about the work that you do at all. I am barely aware of anything other than myself.

The mother says, it's almost impossible for anyone to be aware of anything else except themselves, don't worry.

The son says, I don't know what I am meant to do.

The father says, I don't know what I am meant to do.

The daughter says, I don't know what I am meant to do.

The mother says, never mind.

The four of them continue to eat their breakfast. The radio is on, explaining about what the royals are probably doing right now. The radio is saying how excited the royals must all be and how proud we all are of the wedding.

Hours pass and bliss continues to saturate the house and its occupants. The smell of coronation chicken curls succulently through the atmosphere. Plates are warmed in an oven. Champagne is cooled in a freezer. Messages from work on mobile phones long-ignored, Prudence flutters around the kitchen in a satisfied stupor. Her family occasionally pop their heads round the door and compliment her on the wonderful smells she is making.

The little William and Kate clock on the mantelpiece starts playing God Save the Queen. There is just a quarter of an hour until the wedding begins. The family gather on the sofa in front of the television. They hold Union Jack flags. Four champagne flutes foam in their hands. The father taps out four painkillers into his palm and passes one each to his family members. They place them onto their tongues at the same moment. They swallow them. Delicious champagne to wash it all down.

The ceremony starts on time. The wedding dress is so beautiful that the whole family start to cry. The expressions of love in the eyes of Will and Kate make everyone cry. The chemistry between Kate's sister and Will's brother makes everyone cry. The family's sleeves are all totally saturated in tears as they try desperately to dry their eyes.

Is it like your wedding was? says the son.

Yes, say the mother and father, together. Their synchronicity makes the two of them cry more.

The family hug each other as the ceremony is concluded and they move back into the kitchen for their coronation chicken.

Bobby eats the meal, not thinking once about World of Warcraft or his passionate desire for the female dwarf, or his inability to enjoy his school or any part of his real life in any way. He doesn't care about his feelings of inadequacy or his lack of any social skills. He doesn't care about his violent responses and uncontrollable temper. He doesn't care about not being able to carry out a conversation successfully with anyone who he meets. He doesn't care about anything. I am nothing, he thinks. He is blissfully happy.

Ellen sits and eats the lunch. She is shockingly thin. Her eyes are puffy from crying. There are no messages from Tracy on her mobile phone. She doesn't care that they haven't spoken since they spent the night together. She doesn't care about her poetry or her lovers or her life. She doesn't care about letting people fuck her. She doesn't care about Tracy. She doesn't care that her mother cuts herself and that her father is addicted to painkillers. She doesn't care about anything. I am nothing, she thinks. She is blissfully happy.

Prudence enjoys the taste of the chicken. She has many large cuts on her arms. Some of them are infected and shine red and white in the sun. She doesn't care about not having any identity other than being a wife and a mother. She doesn't care about hating the royal family and wishing that she was allowed to get excited about her own life. She doesn't care that she is completely estranged from her husband and her children and doesn't feel as though she has any relations. She doesn't care about anything. I am nothing, she thinks. She is blissfully happy.

The television presenter eats the coronation chicken with his right hand. His mangled left hand relaxes on the table, bandaged tightly to minimise pain and speed recovery. He doesn't care about the guilt of cheating on his wife with his producer. He doesn't care about being the butt of everyone's jokes. He doesn't care about being the slow one. He doesn't care about being completely estranged from his family. He doesn't care about always working with cars and lads. He doesn't care about his pain. He doesn't care about wanting to be young. He doesn't care about dying. He doesn't care about lust. He doesn't care about feeling trapped. He doesn't care about feeling that every decision he has ever made has been wrong. He doesn't care about feeling like a coward. He doesn't care about anything. I am nothing, he thinks. He is blissfully happy.

The family stand together and sing God Save the Queen. The coronation chicken is delicious.

Acknowledgements

First thanks to Kevin Duffy, my editors Leonora Rustamova and Hetha Duffy and everyone at Bluemoose for their help, encouragement and wisdom.

Thanks to Ben Myers and Adelle Stripe, for recommending me to Bluemoose, and vice-versa.

Thanks to my Metal Man team-mates, Chris Killen and Joe Stretch. My life would be weird and dull without you two.

Thanks to my family, for everything.

Thanks to Crispin Best, Ben Brooks, peterdb, Nick Royle and everyone else who read an early draft of this novel.

Thanks to everyone I work with at Blackwell's.

Final thanks to my girlfriend Red; for your love, patience and belief. I hope we won't have to wait much longer. My life would be miserable without you.